SMALL CAUCASIAN WOMAN

Stories by
Elaine Fowler Palencia

D0067029

University of Missouri Press
Columbia and London

Library of Congress Cataloging-in-Publication Data

Palencia, Elaine Fowler, 1946–
    Small Caucasian woman : stories / by Elaine Fowler Palencia.
    p.   cm.
    ISBN 0-8262-0943-2 (pbk.)
    I. Title.
PS3566.A4584S6   1993
813'.54—dc20   92-46882
                                                              CIP

♾™ This paper meets the requirements of the
American National Standard for Permanence of Paper
for Printed Library Materials, Z39.48, 1984.

Designer: Kristie Lee
Typesetter: Connell-Zeko Type & Graphics
Printer and binder: Thomson-Shore, Inc.
Typefaces: Galliard, ITC Machine, and Basque

To Vanda Galen Botts and Sally Schulzinger,
who have been to Blue Valley.

Contents

Acknowledgments

The author is grateful to the Illinois Arts Council for financial support during the writing of this book, and to the members of the Red Herring Fiction Workshop for their helpful criticism.

The following stories, some under shortened titles, have appeared elsewhere: "What Lee Anne Hawkins Did with Her Life," *Appalachian Heritage;* "Closing Time" and "Flight Out of Egypt," *Blue Moon;* "One Way Out of Here" and "The Biggest Nation," *Crescent Review;* "Pecans," *Farmer's Market;* "The Best-Dressed Man in Dayton," *Gambit;* "Small Caucasian Woman," *Iowa Woman;* "Honey Is Lucky," *Korone;* "What Keeps Shug Watson Going," *Plainswoman;* "The Man I Love," *Sing Heavenly Muse!;* "Thence West to the Place of Beginning," *Wind;* "To Die in Singapore," The Spirit That Moves Us Press's *Free Parking: Fifteenth Anniversary Anthology* (Jackson Heights, Queens, N.Y., 1990).

SMALL CAUCASIAN WOMAN

Prologue

Blanche Callicoat Long Writes an Essay about Blue Valley and the Dark Ages

As the town librarian and archivist of Blue Valley, the county seat of Moore County in eastern Kentucky, I am in a position to know how thoroughly historians have neglected this region. In the large view, the omission is understandable. Little goes on here except what is left out of history books—the seasonal changes of a beautiful natural setting and the joys and sorrows of daily life. Hidden in a labyrinth of narrow valleys and hollows among the foothills of the Appalachians, the town is not on the road to anywhere. To get here, you either have to want to arrive quite badly, or be lost. Except for an early morning ride-through by Morgan's Raiders in 1862, not even the Civil War managed to find it.

The town is isolated by design. In the early 1780s two families, the Farnsworths and the Mosses, came to Kentucky from the Yadkin Valley in what is now North Carolina, where they had been neighbors of Daniel Boone. Finding Fort Boonesborough already too crowded, they and a handful of others followed a buffalo trace into the hills to the northeast, where they founded this town around a salt lick. *The solitude,* wrote Jacob Farnsworth to his brother, *is as fine as that in any village in England.*

1

According to the diary of Joshua Moss, they thought themselves to be the first white settlers in the area, until one spring morning a man and a woman walked out of the woods with a stack of furs to trade. This was Ebenezer Forrester and his Cherokee wife, Tall Susan. For two years they had been living under the rock ledge on Bald Knob. Later, on a hunting expedition, Ebenezer showed the men of the party a limestone wall about thirty feet long, running along Fox Creek in present-day Stonewall Hollow. It was still standing in Mr. Clum Wilson's pasture when I was a child. There were never permanent Indian settlements here; these were hunting grounds only for the Shawnee and the Cherokee. In any case, the Indians are not known to have built such walls. Some say the Vikings got this far. Behind every story whispers another story. Outside the house of recorded history ancient ghosts dance and wave, mocking us.

Within a decade the Farnsworths and Mosses quarreled over the leadership of the community, the first of the family feuds which stereotyped our hills for the rest of the country. Vanquished in the second generation, the Mosses scattered westward with the advancing frontier. The story of one of them, Araminta Moss, survives in a legend of the prairie.

Meanwhile the Farnsworths built the bank, the hotel, the lumber mill, and the railroad. They sent sons to the state legislature, the U.S. Congress, the Union Army, and Yale. They erected on the courthouse lawn a statue commemorating the soldiers of all wars, a monument known locally as King Farnsworth, since its deep-set eyes and shelflike brow are as identifiable with the Farnsworths as the Bourbon nose is with the Bourbons.

But the Farnsworths are merely the aristocracy; and history has belonged to the aristocracy for too long. Blue Valley is a town not of officers, but of foot soldiers. Their lives of quiet perspiration are the rain on the river of history. The individual drops disappear into the flow, but all of them together keep the river from drying up. Though there is more variety in the telephone book than the Anglo-Saxon purists would have you believe—Pennsylvania Dutch Mynhiers, Huguenot DeHarts—a preponderance of surnames derives from the old English occupations: Barber, Baker, Carter, Cooper, Farmer, Hunter, as well as Bowman, an archer, and Fletcher, one who makes arrows. For generations, we have known how things work; and such a hereditary occupational bias may account for our self-reliance and cynicism. A man will work sixteen-hour days to send his son to Blue Valley College, then stand in the back of the auditorium at graduation exercises and scoff, "All that education, and he can't hoe potatoes."

No, formal history will not do at all for Blue Valley.

I have read that every sound that has ever been made is still vibrating in the atmosphere. Someday, when scientists have produced a listening instrument sensitive enough, they will be able to hear the Big Bang. In Blue Valley, we are halfway there already. When I go for my Sunday drive, every bend in the road, every hillside pasture, calls to me, until the voices garble together like faraway radio signals. These are the stories of the land and its people, the history of what has happened on the soil. The only way to untangle the voices is to study gossip.

We are living in the Dark Ages of gossip. Gossiping used to be an honorable calling. It was the author of epic poetry, the godparent of mythology and history. It was the oral tradition. Today, with a satellite dish in the backyard where the outhouse used to be, people are listening to the wrong voices. They know more about what goes on in Knots Landing than they do about the family next door, and in my opinion that's not healthy for either family. I believe that many people with mental and criminal problems today weren't gossiped about enough when they were growing up. When I was in school, we learned a good bit of Robert Burns: "O wad some power the giftie gie us / To see oursels as others see us!" That's what gossip does. Even if it tells a bad story on you, it gives you a story. Without gossip, how would we know who we are?

There are only a few true practitioners of gossip left in the valley. They are as rare as the old men who still know how to sharpen and set the teeth of a handsaw, as anonymous as the bards who taught Homer about Troy. Mostly they talk to each other in order to keep alive their vast and amorphous swirl of stories for the few young who come in search of the past. They are like monks living in obscurity, illuminating the manuscripts of their own minds against that time when the Dark Ages shall lift, and personal history grounded in place becomes important again. I hope I may count myself as one of their disciples.

Reverend Caldwell, our Presbyterian minister, who is no slouch at gossip himself, has remarked that some people are born to gossip; some people achieve mastery of it through hard work; and some have gossiping thrust upon them, by being in the right place at the right time. Working six days a week for the past thirty years in his shoe repair shop on Main Street, my good friend Toy Lewis has traveled all three paths to arrive at his present status of master gossip and unofficial town historian.

Shoe repair, like authentic gossip, is in decline. These days, shoes are more likely to be thrown away than to be repaired. Either they cannot be fixed, being of some man-made material that splits when nailed or resewn, or the repair would cost more than a new, poorly made pair from Brazil. Nevertheless, both Toy's shoe repair and gossip businesses are doing well; for the one reinforces the other. The fact is, people who traffic in the true, context-oriented, genealogically grounded gossip tend to be the same people who wear good leather shoes. Children, teenagers, and flighty people do not appreciate good shoes any more than they appreciate homemade fruitcake. These are mature tastes, requiring a sharp eye to detect imitations, an attention to detail, and a sense of tradition: in short, exactly the qualities necessary to be a good gossiper. Loose-lipped amateurs have given the art a bad name. Among those truly called to the vocation, lying does not exist. The real gossip is compelled to tell the truth as he or she knows it, such truth being subject to continuous revision as more information is acquired. Moreover, the story is never told to the glory of the teller, but only in the service of the greater good. Single-handedly, from behind his scarred counter, Toy Lewis has done more to keep the threads of people's lives interwoven in Blue Valley than anyone else. And this is the greater good: the fabric of the community.

For Toy, no one's story is complete until he has personally seen the second date chiseled on the tombstone. Accompanied by his wife, Nancy, he attends both weddings and funerals; but he prefers funerals. Funerals, says Toy, are more honest. There are fewer promises made at funerals than at weddings, and besides, you can be sure that at least one person, though lying down, isn't lying through his teeth.

Just as Toy saves scraps of leather for odd jobs, so does he save even the most insignificant fact about a person, perhaps for decades, until a use presents itself. Thus when I picked up my newly half-soled brown oxfords at Toy's shop last spring, and mentioned that my husband and I were driving out to Boulder, Colorado, to visit my daughter in graduate school, Toy asked, "Is that anywhere near Denver?" and when I said that it was, he said, "Well, then, that puts me in mind of Iris Randall and that post office business. Doesn't it you?" and he waited patiently while in my mind I went down and down the corridor of years to an age-warped door and opened it and looked and thought and said, "Toy, do you really, actually, think, after all this time—?" and Toy spat tobacco juice into a coffee can and returned, "Well, might could be. They might be another layer to it, if you had the time to go look."

One thing Toy and I have commented on is that old stories tend to have layers, like an archaeological site. The first layer of Iris Randall's story, the only one that was widely known, was laid down in 1913, the year of the Great Pear Ridge Revival. Iris was fifteen then, one of four daughters and six sons of Zebediah and Levisa Jane Randall who lived in a two-story log house on the Breathitt's Mill Road. During a mass baptism in the Elliott Creek swimming hole, Iris caught a cold. Walking to school in the early fall rains during her "monthlies" brought on consumption and she was sent to a sanatorium in faraway Denver. There she died within a few weeks and was buried without any of her family in attendance. That would have been the only layer, except that during the nineteen thirties, a second layer was scratched in what Toy calls "the post office business." In that decade Toy's uncle became a rural mail carrier over in Douthit, two post offices from where the Randalls lived. There, upon three different occasions, he observed Iris's mother surreptitiously mailing packages to Denver.

Although Zebediah and Levisa Randall maintained until their deaths that Iris had died in 1913, though all their children believed it, and though no one else in Blue Valley ever had any reason to doubt that finality, Toy, through his superior gossiping instincts and mysterious contacts, was able to excavate further. So that the day I interrupted my visit with my daughter in Boulder and drove down to Denver alone, I knew that the preacher at the Great Pear Ridge Revival, Iris's charismatic, forty-year-old uncle Hampton "Hamp" Randall, had gone to Denver with her. Far from having tuberculosis, she was pregnant with the first of the three blind children she would bear him. When their fourth child was born sighted but with a congenital heart problem that took the infant at eighteen months, Hamp, convinced that the Lord had forsaken him, climbed into the bathtub with his shotgun, put the barrel in his mouth, and pulled the trigger.

But he was still listed in the Denver phonebook these many years later, and the woman who answered the phone was his daughter. When I told her where I was from and that my daddy's people were related to Iris's mother, she invited me to stop by.

Leah Randall met me at the door of a graying, asbestos-shingled bungalow in a weedy, dying neighborhood. In her early seventies and stone-blind, she sat me down in a sparsely furnished living room, served me lemonade and vanilla wafers, and volunteered that she had worked as a switchboard operator in an office building until she retired. None of her brothers and sisters had lived to adulthood.

I explained a little more about my mission and how Toy and I had just thought that whoever was left might like to see someone from home.

"Mother always talked about how good the cornbread was on the farm. They took their own corn to be ground at the mill," she said. "She'll want to see you just for a minute. She's not really strong enough for company. She still has her mind but I hope you understand that old people get certain ideas sometimes, and can't let go of them."

She led the way to a back room bright with late sun, where an incredibly old woman lay in a white iron bed, a woman of such fragility, with an aureole of wispy white hair and finely wrinkled parchment skin, that I was reminded of a puff from a milkweed pod and fancied that the faded quilt had been spread over Iris to keep her from blowing away.

Leah said, "Mother, this is Blanche Long. We've been talking about the old times and having a good visit."

Iris's gaze drifted to her daughter. "Did you tell her the truth?"

"Now, Mother, that doesn't matter anymore," Leah soothed her.

Iris's sparrow-claw hands plucked randomly at the quilt. All of a sudden she raised up and stared at me. "Hit were the sheep's eyes. I've studied and studied on it since Hamp died. Hit weren't him being my uncle. That's in the Bible all over, a man and his niece. Hamp could quote chapter and verse on that. Hit were the sheep he sheared before I knew him, when he was working for a man named Barnes. To keep them still, Hamp'd press on their eyelids. There was the cause of all our troubles. Tell Sadie and Sarah and Bithie . . . Clinton and Garland. . . ."

She sank back on her pillow, her skin as thin over her skull as the skin on a pan of scalded milk. Leah touched my elbow to go.

At the front door she said, "Mother always believed that someday she'd get to tell that to someone from home. She'll rest easy now."

When I got back to Blue Valley three weeks later, I of course told all of this to Toy Lewis.

When I had finished, he nodded. "I figured you found Iris, because the day before you got home, young Mayor Hogge come in the shoe shop wanting to know who exactly was Iris Randall. His office received word from a daughter in Denver to notify any living kin in Moore County that Iris had died."

"Do you think maybe somebody should have been sent to Iris earlier, so she could have died in peace a lot sooner?" I wondered.

Toy said, "No, that would be too forward. Blue Valley people cannot abide a forward person. It had to be done sort of by the way or Iris wouldn't have talked."

And of course Toy is right.

Though Iris had long since accepted her physical exile, she wanted to be brought back home in the form of her own explanation of her life. Toy and I have done that for her. Now she will outlast much of what she knew here. After all, in 1960 Mr. Clum Wilson tore down the prehistoric wall in his pasture and used the rock for a road to his new pond. The salt lick around which Blue Valley was founded lies under the parking lot of the mini-mall, where the concrete has sunk in the middle. It's a puzzle, says Toy. Nothing ever happens here. You feel like you see the same old people day after day. And yet, things aren't like they used to be, and a lot of the people you find yourself talking to when you're alone are for one reason or another not actually walking these streets. It's enough to make you think, says he, that we're making up an awful lot of life as we go along; that Blue Valley may, in fact, be largely a state of mind; and what worries him is, if the day comes when nobody knows the stories that make it Blue Valley anymore, and nobody's actively thinking about it, well—then he laughs and turns red, embarrassed to be talking such foolishness. He puts another shoe on the last, positions a nail on the sole, and hits it extra hard with his hammer, as if to assure himself that he's still there.

The Best-Dressed Man in Dayton

This happened over forty years ago, when I was twice as dumb as I look. I'll tell it while he's out getting cigarettes. Hell, it won't kill anything if he walks in. When Floyd knows Dreama's been drinking, he doesn't listen to a word I say.

But see, it was tough on the farm. We worked sixteen hours a day, six days a week. If we had time off, there was no place to go but church or the beer joint. Mom went to church, Randall snuck to the beer joint, Norton locked himself in his room reading books, and Dad stayed outside, working anyway or beating the mules. They kept me hard at the housework and never let me go anywhere but to church or school. Everybody in the hollow lived this hard way except the Flannerys, that were so lazy they wouldn't work in a pie factory. The summer I was sixteen I wrote to my Aunt Sadie, that lived up in Sidney, and told her how it was. The next week she sent me twenty dollars. Not long after that I got Mom to let me go across the river and visit my friend Piggy Dalton, at the same time that Piggy got her mother to let her come and visit me. We met on her side of the river and run away together on the bus to Cincinnati.

In Cincinnati a truck-driver cousin of Piggy's and his wife got us work in an amusement park and helped us find a rented room. Next time he made a run out of town, I had him take along a postcard from me to Mom and Dad, saying I was all right. He mailed it from Oklahoma City.

Piggy took tickets on the Loop-the-Loop and I worked at a diner on the midway, where I got acquainted with everybody: the snake lady, the world's fattest twins, the strong man—I wrote to him for years after he went to prison. At night eating cheese and crackers in our room, Piggy would say, "Ain't this the life? I'm

9

never going back," and I'd say, "Only way you'd get me to go home would be to ship me back dead in a pine box. And when it got there and they opened it, I wouldn't be in it!"

One evening after we'd been there about three weeks, it was around the end of July, this dude come in and set down in my section. You wouldn't think so to look at him now, but every woman in the place turned to stare at him: hair slicked back like George Raft, two-tone shoes, and a three-piece suit. When I went to lay down his silverware, his big brown eyes ran over me like beetles.

"You're new here. What's your name?"

"Dreama Forrester."

"Floyd McDonald. I run the novelty stand over by the racetrack."

I couldn't help asking, "How's come you dress like you do? Nobody else that works here does."

He spread his fingers out like two fans of playing cards and admired his ring. It had a gold horseshoe set with diamonds on it. "Floyd McDonald's just my nickname. What they really call me up home is, the Best-Dressed Man in Dayton." While I was marveling at this, he said in a louder voice, "Give me the fried chicken special. A breast and the left drumstick. Make sure it's the left, now."

"You just want the left one?"

"You got some, ain't you?"

"Why, I don't know," I said.

"Whaddya mean, you don't know? Go ask the cook," he said.

When I come back from the kitchen, half the restaurant was waiting to hear.

"We can't tell the difference. What is it?" I said.

He looked all around the restaurant, drawing everybody in. "Well, when a chicken sleeps, it stands on its right leg. That makes the right one tough. So you only want to eat the left one, right? I'd think somebody fresh off the farm'd know that."

Now, Forresters is tough. You can chew our arm off and we won't shed a tear. But after him getting the whole place to laugh at me, I wouldn't go near him for nothing in this world. I give Maureen, the other waitress, fifty cents to switch sections until he left.

Yet I kept thinking about his good looks and smooth talk. On payday, I bought me this black dress with big white polka dots, that had a circle skirt and a red stretch belt with a rhinestone buckle. After work I got Piggy to walk home with me a different way, past the racetrack. Sure enough, there he was in a suit the color of vanilla ice cream, convincing about a dozen people to buy two kewpie dolls and get a free whoopee cushion. I linked my arm through Piggy's and put a little extra in my walk.

"Hey, farmer!" he yelled.

I just kept going, talking to Piggy.

"Hey! Farmer!"

The next day he come in and set down in Maureen's section like he didn't know me. I acted the same, until directly I noticed he was rolling quarters down his arm. While he was waiting for his pie, he done a whole roll that way, balancing each one on his shoulder and letting it roll right down off his fingertips and into an ashtray. And the nearer he got to the end of the roll, the nearer I got to him. When the last quarter hit the ashtray, without even looking up he said, "When do you get off work, Dreama Forrester?"

That evening he took me to a place called Charlie O'Day's. The minute we walked in, the band switched to "Teddy Bears' Picnic," which turned out to be Floyd's theme song. He got up on that bandstand and pretended to play every single instrument. I never had such a time in my life, and I didn't even drink in those days. Didn't need to, then.

After that we'd go out two or three times a week, and every time was better than the last. Once we went to eat Italian with friends of his. Lord, everybody was his friend: he wasn't like me, that only had the friends I was born with. It was a real fancy place and they said we'd have to wait two hours for a table. But Floyd got hold of the maître d', slipped him some money, and told him we was on our honeymoon. In ten minutes we had a table with complimentary appetizers. It seemed like he could solve any problem. And when we went dancing, he'd dance with his hat on, and every once in a while he'd stop in the middle of the floor and balance his hat on his toe. Then he'd give this little kick and it would sail up and land right on his head. People would clap and I'd tell myself, look what you'd be missing if you'd stayed on that farm.

The only trouble was, the time I was spending with Floyd cut into my time with Piggy. I didn't notice until later, but she was getting quieter and fatter. One evening she wasn't waiting by the gates to walk home with me. When I got back to our room, there was a note saying she'd gone back home to help her family strip tobacco and she hoped I curled up and died.

What would you do, sixteen years old and alone in the evil city? I went over to the sink in the corner and coughed up everything but my toenails. Then I dressed for my date that night with Floyd and laid down on the bed. My dreams of glory was over. Not no way could I pay the rent without Piggy's half. Besides, somebody might climb up the drainspout and slit my throat while I slept, and I wouldn't even know who his people were. Yet if I went home, Mom and Dad would beat the tar out of me and then everybody would say I had went to sin and nobody would marry me. That would be the end, because I wasn't smart enough to be an old maid schoolteacher. Then I thought, Floyd will know what to do. He knows everything.

When he come to pick me up, he had on a new pinstripe suit, with a big ruby stickpin in his tie. Before I could say a word, he hustled me out to a taxi that had two other couples in the back.

"These're my new friends and we feel lucky tonight!" he told me.

One of the women threw her head back and whooped. What you call a suicide blond: dyed by her own hand.

I said, "I'm glad to be with a cheerful crowd. It's just what I need tonight."

"Oh, we're cheerful all right. Didn't get these red noses in the Chicago fire!" the other woman laughed. She had a black saucer hat tilted over one eye and little pointed cat teeth.

The man with her said, "Robbing the cradle, ain't you, Pappy?" and everybody thought that was so funny that for the rest of the evening Floyd's name was Pappy. The other person was a big bruiser they called Hammer.

I was setting up front with Floyd, and the first chance I got, I whispered, "Guess what: Piggy went home."

"Yeah?" He turned around to Hammer. "Listen to this," he said, and he told the one about the farmer's daughter and the duck.

"I don't think you understand," I said when everybody was done laughing. "I can't stay in Cincinnati by myself. It ain't re-spectable and I can't afford it. What'm I going to do?"

"Do-wacka-do. Hey, you guys, reach me that bottle," he said. I grabbed onto his sleeve. "You've got to think of something. You don't want me to go back home, do you?" He looked at me sideways out of one eye, the way a rooster will do. "Say. I was going to wear my black and white shoes tonight, but I couldn't find the black one."

"Floyd, be serious!" I begged.

The backseaters broke up and one of the women yelled, "Ooh, Pappy, it's going to be a long night!"

Floyd swore and pulled a roll of bills out of his pocket. "See this, Dream'? I'm going to double this tonight. Right over there! That's the bridge to Newport. Hell, we might even go to California after this. How'd you like that? Not no need to worry when you're with the Best-Dressed Man in Dayton! Ain't that what they call me?"

"They do, Pappy!" the women shouted.

For a little, I did forget my troubles as I looked at those Ohio River bridge lights hanging in the night. I recalled what I'd heard about Newport around the diner: about the casinos and the big-name entertainers, the fancy restaurants and the dark-complected men that ran things, and about the bodies found in alleys. The big time at last, I thought. My purse and my shoes match, and I'm with the Best-Dressed Man in Dayton. Plus we must be engaged if he's taking me to California.

We went to all the famous places, like the Beverly Hills Club and the Lookout House. We lost track of one couple but Floyd wired into a different crowd that took us to the casino at the Blue Shamrock. There he settled down at a card game where he seemed to know a man. I thought, here's where I learn how Floyd's going to make us rich, so I kept quiet and watched every little thing. But when I whispered to him, "Why do you keep pulling on your ear lobe? Do you have an itch?" he give me a handful of change and told me to go play the jukebox in the bar.

After a while he come after me. "Give me your money," he said.

"You've got plenty of money. I seen it," I said.

"I want to double yours too. Hand it over," he said, grinning back along his teeth like an alligator.

I give him all the folding kind, imagining the fur coat I'd buy. After that I must have played every song in that jukebox once and the Guy Lombardo ones twice. My change was running low and a busboy was stacking chairs when the bartender come over.

"Are you waiting for somebody?"

"Yes, my fiancé's in there playing cards," I said.

"The card room closed half an hour ago. Maybe you'd like me to call you a cab," he said. He was an older man, well-spoken like Uncle Coke.

I said, "I reckon it's just taking him a long time to count his money. He's taking me to Hollywood on it."

The bartender sighed. "That man that was in here earlier: Floyd McDonald. That's your fiancé?"

"That's him."

He went to the telephone behind the bar. "The cab'll be here in five minutes."

"Then I'll round up Floyd," I said. "Maybe he'll want to buy the taxi."

The place was huge, room after room of chandeliers and red brocade drapes and such. None of the few people wandering around the kitchen knew where Floyd was. Once I saw Hammer go by a doorway like he was looking for somebody too, but he disappeared before I could speak to him. Directly, backstage of the nightclub part, I run onto a little hall. It was dark as the inside of a boot, except for a little bit of light showing under a door at the end. Behind the door, a man was crying. I'd never heard a man cry before, except when Lon Eldridge was moved to testify at revivals. That was happy crying, though. This crying was blubbery and scared.

"Don't mess up my face, please don't mess up my face," the crier said, and it was Floyd.

"That ain't all I'm going to mess up," a big mean voice said. Then come a scuffling sound and it added, "And that goes for you too. You're next."

"This ain't what it looks like!" a woman wailed.

There was a thud and Floyd's voice went up a notch. "Jesus, not my face—!"

I come barreling through the door.

It was a kind of a storeroom, jumbled with barstools and desks and lamps and cocktail tables. Smack in front of me, Hammer had

Floyd around the neck with one hand. The other was raised to clobber him again. Floyd's lip was cut and his pants was nowhere in sight. Over to one side the suicide blond huddled naked on a mattress, holding an aluminum tray in front of her. When Hammer turned to see who'd busted in, Floyd jerked loose and went hopping behind an armchair. Realizing it was me, he bawled, "I'm drunk, I'm drunk, I don't know what I'm doing."

"*She* knows what *she's* doing, the two-timing bitch!" Hammer bellowed, and he went for the blond.

Part of me wanted to finish the job on Floyd and then scratch the blond's eyes out. But I'm an underdog person, no matter what the situation. Hammer must have weighed two-thirty, but I jumped right in front of him.

"Back up and push," I said. "These hands is strong from wringing out wet overalls. Fourteen-ounce denim. And I can turn any jar lid off, even if it breaks the jar."

"Get outta the way, kid!" he roared and swept me aside like I was a fly.

The blond grabbed up her clothes and flew out the door.

Out he went after her. There was a crash in the hall and screaming, then sobs and a dragging sound going off toward the casino.

When I turned around, Floyd was setting in the chair trying to put his shoes on. He kept missing the shoe with his foot.

I went to help the fool. When I knelt down, my knees give way and I started shaking.

He laid his hand gently on my head. In a little while he started stroking my hair, soft and trembly. "I'm sorry, honey, I'm sorry. There must've been something funny in that whiskey, it got me so confused. She's nothing. You're the only one I love."

"You love me?" I said.

"I swear to God."

I kept busy with his shoes. Nobody had ever touched me gently like that, except once when I had pneumonia and Dad set by my bed a few minutes, patting my hand. Nobody had ever said they loved me. Forresters is the type to wait until after you're dead to say it. I looked down at the foot in my hand. It was as narrow as a girl's, with a high, delicate arch. It could never stand all day in a field hoeing corn, no more than his hands could swing an ax.

These was dancing feet, card-playing hands. They would never be nothing else. As for what Floyd had just got involved in, I asked myself what else I could have expected. Men were children, every one of them. Except not as cute.

He doubled over. "I'm sick, oh, I'm sick."

"Dreama'll take care of you. Mama'll take you home," I said, as I seen my future rise up before me like a rainbow.

We had to walk the whole three miles back to Cincinnati on account of Floyd lost all our money at the card game. On the bridge I had a moment when I looked upriver toward home. It occurred to me that a few hours before, the water that was flowing under us now had trickled down the watercress-choked creek behind the farm, maybe about the time that Mom was putting supper on the table and the hydrangeas by the kitchen door was glowing white like globe lights in the dusk. And now they were all asleep, with the breeze off the river stirring the curtains where Randall snored in the little room off the kitchen, where Mom and Dad slept under Grandma Rossiter's quilt, and upstairs Norton dreamed of the knights and damsels in his storybooks. Then I recollected Lot's wife and set my face forward again.

I took him to my room, and of course in those days if a man spent the night in your room and you were respectable to start with, you could get him to marry you. So the next week we tied the knot up in Sidney, with Aunt Sadie looking on. When we went out to eat after the wedding, Floyd won ten dollars from a man who said he couldn't drop-kick a cigarette and have it land in his mouth. Which Floyd did, with the cigarette lit. He was the life of the party then, but now the music's a little fast for him. It was when we got the marriage license that I found out how old he really was, but I've always kept him dressed young and I see that he takes all his pills.

See, I figure that the point of it all is survival. It turned out that he didn't like to work much. But we're still together. I never had to go back to the farm. Sure, we've missed a meal or two, and sure, there was that woman up in Dayton. But when I found out about her, I just paid her a visit with a can of red lye in my hand. "You'll never look at him again with this thrown in your eyes," I said, and that was that. Whereas Piggy was the one ended up an old maid, working in a shirt factory until she died of the sugar. Hammer's gone. The suicide blond, who knows? She was the type to get shot arguing over whether a doughnut hole is the hole in the middle of the doughnut or the piece of dough that's taken out of the hole. So my advice to the young girls is this: A woman's got to have broad shoulders to be married. No matter what else goes, keep your teeth and your hair. Check through his pockets at night and throw away all the phone numbers; they won't do either one of you any good. Keep an h.o.—that's a holdout of emergency money he don't know about. And it won't hurt to love him. You'll get a nice surprise once in a while to keep you going. For instance, it turns out that mine fries the best egg you ever ate.

Pecans

I was sitting with a book in my lap and a drink at my elbow when my brother phoned to tell me he was twenty miles from the house and he had pecans.

"Frankie. Well. It must be three years. Where do you live now?" I said.

"All that can keep. You still in the gray house?" he said, with a new accent I placed as maybe Texan.

Our father was born here. A Farnsworth has always lived in it.

"Do the Windsors still live in that castle," I said.

I made myself another drink and sat back down with the book. But with company coming it seemed like I ought to do more, so I got up and opened a box of baking soda and put it in the refrigerator.

In a little while I heard a car in the street. I changed the TV from the soap to a movie on the Arts & Entertainment network and stepped out on the porch.

Frankie was driving an old black Ford with all the windows rolled down, no hubcaps, and two passengers. He was deeply tanned and sported a Pancho Villa moustache and shoulder-length hair. There seemed to be some confusion about his getting out of the car, and when he finally made it I could see why. He was on crutches and his left leg was bandaged and splinted from the ankle to the top of his thigh. Driving in that condition would be an interesting proposition. He was about twenty pounds heavier than I remembered him. A blond woman got out of the passenger side and went around to steady him. Right behind her a little blond girl bounced out of the back seat carrying an Alf doll upside down.

"Hi, Wart," said Frankie.

"Rufus," I said.

18

Frankie said, "This's my sister Sherry. Sherry, this's Teresa and this is Starlight."

"Hi. These are for you," said Teresa, and handed me a grocery sack of unshelled pecans. Like Frankie she was very tan. She wore panty-length cutoffs, a faded tank top, and rubber thong sandals. She had the small, flat body of an eleven-year-old tomboy, but the lines around her eyes were much, much older. Starlight was maybe three or four and wore a lavender playsuit with mustard stains down the front.

"We'll shell the pecans after dinner so Teresa can make you a pecan pie. She's great at it, a great piemaker," Frankie said as he struggled into the house.

"So what happened to you?" I asked, when he had let himself down on the sofa, with Teresa and Starlight on either side of him.

"Asshole hit me broadside on my motorcycle," said Frankie.

Teresa said, "He was thrown twenty-nine feet and landed with his head wedged in the gutter, no helmet." She took a thick packet of photographs out of her purse, slipped off the rubber band, and passed them to me one at a time. "This one was taken in the emergency room. You can see the blood trickling out of his ear. In this one you can see this major hematoma on his right leg. He's got a pin in his hip, you know."

"Teresa used to work in the same hospital. It's amazing," Frankie said. Frankie, who, like all the Farnsworths, is incapable of amazement.

"Where was it you two met?" I asked.

Teresa winked at Frankie. "We met Elsewhere. Didn't we?"

Frankie grinned and pinched her thigh. Nor are we pinchers.

"Maybe you'd like something to drink," I offered.

Frankie glanced at Teresa. "Got any longnecks?"

"He's not supposed to have alcohol on account of his head injury," Teresa informed me with a sigh.

"And that one," Frankie pointed a finger at Teresa, "can't have any cigarettes. She's trying to quit."

Teresa leaned provocatively toward him, her small breasts doing their best to spill out of her tank top. "You mean you're trying to *make* me quit."

"I'll do it, too," he said.

"And I'll put your nose in a splint," she said and went kiss-kiss at him.

In a loud voice Starlight said, "I want *ice* cream."

I considered getting up but I'd just done that, so I waved in the direction of the kitchen.

Frankie and Teresa went in there and rattled around in the refrigerator and the cabinets. Much giggling transpired. While they were gone I changed the TV to cartoons. Starlight scooted over to sit cross-legged on the floor about two feet from the screen, cradling her Alf doll. When Frankie and Teresa returned, he was carrying a glass of club soda and she had a bottle of Pepsi for herself and a glass of Pepsi with ice for Starlight.

"So," I said.

"So . . . what are the chances of getting a nap before dinner? That was a twenty-hour drive," Frankie said.

"Don't feel like talking?" I said.

Frankie's eyes swept the bare mantel. "Do you?"

I gave them the master bedroom, and as soon as they finished their drinks they went upstairs. Starlight continued to watch cartoons. Every once in a while she turned Alf over and spanked him. "Don't ever try to leave me, bitch. I've got a gun," she warned Alf. "Leave the quaaludes out of this."

About seven, just after I'd discovered some steaks in the freezer, Teresa came downstairs and stared out the window over the sink for a while. She had the clear, steady gaze of the sincerely stupid.

"You've got a nice yard," she said. "I think I'll go look at it."

She went down under the trees and wormed a squashed pack of cigarettes out of her cutoffs. Leaning against the walnut tree, she rapidly smoked two of them.

I imagined how nice everyone would be to her if she came to one of our family Christmas dinners, Cousin Adele all in purple at the head of the table graciously chatting with her about the heaviness of the silverware and the pre–Civil War construction of the mansion; the Governor's silly sister inviting Teresa to see her horse farm and immediately forgetting she had; Uncle Edward ponderously retelling how Jacob Farnsworth and Joshua Moss founded Blue Valley. Only Mary Alice's husband, Kevin, would cut her, because he knows he will never be one of us.

After supper was cleared away, I found a nutcracker and a set of picks, relics from some long-gone holiday season, and Frankie dumped the sack of pecans on the kitchen table. He cracked them; Teresa and I picked. Starlight fell asleep on the sofa with her thumb in her mouth. While we worked I told them that Mother was going to be in *Blithe Spirit* in Seattle in the fall, and that Dad had married the little Italian actress and was currently directing *Cherry Orchard* in Toronto. I described a new French play I went to see Mother do in upstate New York a couple of years ago.

"She keeps a tennis trophy of yours on display in her dressing room. She loves for people to ask about it," I told Frankie.

"Yeah, which one?" he asked.

"The one from the City Open, the year you were at Yale."

"Ah," said Frankie. "Those were the days, my friend."

"You did it all," I said.

"No, there was one thing I never got to do. Never was allowed to do. You weren't either," said Frankie.

"Fail," I said, and he nodded.

"Frankie and me are going to school," said Teresa. "Did he tell you? The Walker Technical Institute? In Corsicana? Computers are the thing now."

"*You're* studying computers?" I asked.

She popped a pecan half in her mouth. "No, Frankie is. He got the highest entrance score they'd ever had. When he told me what it was, I was like, *whoa.*"

"Teresa's studying to be a commercial artist," said Frankie, concentrating hard on his task. "She drew these pictures of cowboys and Indians for her sister's kids. They've got them framed and hanging in the bedrooms."

"Frankie says I can draw a horse so real you could ride it," said Teresa, making her shoulders strut. When we had enough nutmeats for two pies, we called it quits.

In the mornings, when Frankie was full of energy, he and Teresa did errands. One day they brought in a mud-caked pile of sheets and blankets and spent the morning washing and folding. Another morning they took the Ford to a car wash. A different time they took off to buy tampons and were gone three hours. That day when they came back Teresa said, "Why didn't somebody tell me there was a frigging statue of your great-grandfather in front of the courthouse?"

From time to time they borrowed money from me and bought groceries. By lunchtime Frankie's face would be jaundiced and there would be olive bruises under his eyes. Generally he disappeared upstairs until suppertime. This schedule gave the two of us no time alone. While he was upstairs I sat on the couch reading. Teresa watched TV and nursed the Pepsi she had started at breakfast. One afternoon Oprah had psychologists on.

"My husband was studying psychology. I've been analyzed through every orifice of my body," Teresa said.

Starlight, who was propped up among the sofa pillows like a stuffed animal, gave Alf a wallop. "Bad Billy! I'll smack your booty!"

"Billy, that's my seven-year-old. My husband's got him somewhere," said Teresa. "At least, he'd be seven by now."

One afternoon she excused herself to go to the bathroom and in the hall mirror I saw her slip money out of my purse. She left by the back door, ran down the yard, and went over the board fence like a squirrel. Due to Uncle Bud's greed there was a commercial strip on the other side now, tavern, gas station, pet shop, discount furniture store, Social Security office. In a little while she shinnied back over, a pack of cigarettes in her teeth. She climbed up in a tree and lit one.

Frankie came downstairs early, just as she was returning.

"Sherry's as big a reader as you, Frankie," Teresa said brightly. "She reads all day long."

I looked down at the book in my lap. It appeared to be a college biology text.

"Frankie reads all the time. He'll stay in a bookstore till I'm ready to pee my pants," said Teresa. She climbed behind him and sat on the back of the sofa to massage his shoulders. Frankie winced and closed his eyes. "Remember that one book I read, honey?"

"Tell Sherry about your book," said Frankie, eyes still closed.

"I had to send for it. It's a TV offer, which you cannot buy it in any store," said Teresa. "There is a race of UFOs living five miles under Antarctica. They are who is taking care of the world. This woman in Oklahoma wrote about them."

"I guess I missed reading about them in the paper," I said, staring at Frankie, who knew through his closed lids that I was looking at him.

"Oh, you wouldn't read about them in the newspaper. The Army is hushing it up. Like they did with the one they captured in Mesa, Arizona, in 1948," said Teresa. "Nobody sure ever saw him again."

"What do they look like?" I asked.

"Tall and blond," said Frankie. "Tall and blond."

"Blue eyes," I said.

"Blue eyes," said Frankie, and opened his.

That night he marinated chicken parts in some concoction involving soy sauce and black coffee and we barbecued them. We had pecan pie for dessert.

"It's very good, delicious. Although we didn't grow up eating sweets," I told Teresa.

"That was your mistake. I make Frankie a pie nearly every day. The sugar rush is what keeps me going and he says I'm a survivor," said Teresa.

About two-thirty in the morning I went down to the kitchen without turning any lights on and poured myself a glass of orange juice. I was adding to it when Frankie's voice came from the living room.

"What's that you're putting in?"

"Vodka." In the light from the street, I could see him on the sofa.

"Hit me," he said, holding out his glass, and I poured a cool silver core of vodka into the center of the beer.

We drank in silence for a while. Then I said, "I'm going to tell you this because I'm family. Do you know how to make pecan pie? You make the crust, put it in the pan, and sprinkle one and one-half cups of pecans over it. Then you beat up eggs, sugar, corn syrup, melted butter, and vanilla, and you pour that over the pecans. That's all there is to it. She made the filling today, Frankie, and then she said to me, 'Where are the crusts? Don't you have any in the freezer?' Now *you* tell *me:* What kind of a great piemaker doesn't even know how to make the crust? That's the only skill part. She can't even make goddamn piecrust."

Frankie ran his finger around the rim of his glass. "She could learn. You could teach her."

I didn't answer that and he said, "The other guy died, you know."

"What other guy?"

"The guy that was riding behind me on my bike."

"Who was he?"

"My best friend," said Frankie.

So now I could see why he hadn't bothered to ask why Mamie wasn't cooking for me anymore or why I was no longer working, or where Howard and the children were.

"You're not the only relative I have. And the whole trunk of the car is full of pecans," said Frankie.

Blanche Long Recalls What Lee Anne Hawkins Did with Her Life

If you've ever been in the office at the shirt factory, you've probably seen Lee Anne Hawkins's graduation picture. It sits in the glass display case by the door, along with her Best Student Award and the softball trophies won by the company team.

Maybe you even remember when Lee Anne herself used to play under those big trees out front, making acorn dolls and drawing pictures on cardboard shirt inserts while she waited for her mother's shift to end. In those days old Mr. Tanner was still running things, and it amused him the way Lee Anne would sing out "Hello, Mr. Eldon Tanner Senior!" as he was leaving at the end of the day. He would holler something back as he walked to his car, like asking what game she was playing, and one time Lee Anne shouted back that she was counting her money. She was about the age of his grandchildren, so he strolled over to see. Lee Anne showed him a pile of acorn caps that she said were dimes, some acorn nuts that were her nickels, and a bunch of pebbles that served for quarters. She was barely in school and small for her age. Mr. Tanner was so tickled by how tiny and serious she was that he pulled out several coins and told her that if she could tell him how much they totaled, she could have them all. Now, Lee Anne had helped her Grandpa Hawkins at his roadside vegetable stand, so she counted up that change like a cash register. After that, Mr. Tanner would call out a simple addition or subtraction problem whenever he saw her, and if

Lee Anne got it right, he'd give her a quarter and tell whoever might be passing that he was training her to be his payroll clerk.

Lee Anne's mother, Ada, and two of Ada's sisters had each started working at the factory when they finished the eighth grade, and they were proud as they could be of the way Lee Anne came up with those right answers for an important man like Mr. Tanner. They even started saying within the family that maybe Lee Anne could grow up to be the payroll clerk for real. It was the highest post they could imagine any ordinary person attaining: a clean job away from machines, and having to do with the most important part of people's lives, their salaries.

The Hawkinses lived in a trailer out on Elliott Creek, but with Lee Anne showing so much promise, they decided to move to town so that she could have the advantages. They rented a little house on Second Street and enrolled Lee Anne in the college lab school, which charged a stiff tuition. Almost no county kids went there; it was twelve grades of town kids, a good part of them from faculty families. Ada worked overtime whenever she could and Buell, Lee Anne's daddy, took to fixing cars in their backyard after he got off work at the Ford garage. In the summers he would enter demolition derbies at the various county fairs to bring in a little more extra. His sister, who worked at the laundry, made Lee Anne the most beautiful school clothes out of unclaimed dry cleaning.

I understand that in France villages are known for their vineyards and in England, for the age of their churches. Around here, towns are known for their high school stars. Mostly that means the homecoming queens and the basketball teams, but an excellent student can reach almost the same level of renown. The town owns these high school stars the way that a voting district owns its state representative: you do what you do not for yourself or even for your school, but for everybody, old and young. Early on, people knew that Lee Anne was destined to be a star. Not only was she smart, but she lived with great seriousness, as if in grade school she already had a high, secret goal. People rallied around. By the time she was in the fourth grade, she was taking math with the sixth graders, and the high school French teacher was tutoring her in French on Saturdays. Each week her neighbor, Miss Portia Sophia Jefferson, invited her over to watch "The $64,000 Question," even though Miss Jefferson thinks there are far too many children in the world. Every time Lee Anne got a right answer, Miss Jefferson would give her two chocolate-covered raisins. Even Lee Anne's daddy got into the act, teaching her what he knew best. At twelve Lee Anne was roaring around the back roads in that old Mercury of his with the oversized engine and, so they say, the concealed tanks for running moonshine, which he later used to get money for her college expenses. Buell was good, but he always said that Lee Anne had better driving reflexes than he did. All the hard work paid off. On her college entrance exams Lee Anne made the highest scores in the high school's history, including the scores of Little Tom Draper, whose IQ improved so dramatically after his father, Big Tom, became principal. Naturally the boys didn't want to date a brain like Lee Anne, but Mrs. DeHart the guidance counselor, who takes personal credit for the marriage of thirty-two high school couples during her counseling career, always saw that Lee Anne had an escort for the big dances.

About the only relief Lee Anne got from achievement was the time she spent with her grandparents up Stonewall Hollow. Besides farming, her Grandpa Hawkins played the fiddle for local square dances. He taught Lee Anne to accompany him a little on the guitar, just for porch-playing. Granny Hawkins wove clothing out of dog hair: mittens, hats, purses, scarves. Given the right dog they look like angora; and they're warmer than sheep's wool. The only drawback is that if you're wearing them and get caught in the rain, you smell like wet dog. Granny Hawkins may still be alive. Those little dried-up, pruny women last forever; and besides, in Blue Valley the dead tend to linger. That is, the daily routine is so regular and you get so used to seeing the same people in the same places, that it's hard to be sure exactly when they depart. People on Mr. Mauk's street heard his cane tapping down the sidewalk on his evening constitutional for a year after he died. The young deaths, of course, are different. Those you remember.

The first anybody knew of Lee Anne going to that fancy private college so far away was when Buell asked Big Tom Draper, while he was gassing up Big Tom's car, if he'd ever heard of it. The school was Adele Farnsworth's idea. Adele hardly speaks to anybody but Pascal Dupre, members of the Booklovers Club, and the Governor's sister, but this was a question of Blue Valley being represented in the outside world. For years Adele had been on the lookout for someone she could send to her alma mater, especially after Doctor Tate's girls turned out to be too stupid. Now she took Lee Anne shopping for the right clothes and got in touch with her old sorority. Not that Adele paid for the clothes, mind you. The tightest people in this town are the ones with old money. But Eldon Tanner Junior—the old man had passed away—established the Tanner Shirt scholarship to take care of her tuition. That scholarship is still awarded every year at high school commencement.

Lee Anne left for college in Blue Valley's first Volvo, which on Adele's advice Buell somehow got through his garage connections. Having a car allowed Lee Anne to get to and from college on her own. Her parents never visited her there. Buell said that Ada couldn't get off from work; while Ada said that Buell couldn't.

Lee Anne did well at college. She pledged Adele's sorority and became pretty instead of just pleasant-looking. In the summers she still cashiered at the picture show and she was still friendly to everybody, but people said she wasn't a Blue Valley girl anymore. For one thing, now that the boys she had gone to school with were actually calling her up for dates, she wasn't interested. She only dated Dr. Caldwell's son, who had been at military school since he was ten and really wasn't a native anymore. The girls she had been friends with felt that they and Lee Anne no longer had much in common. But everybody understood that it was to be expected. Wasn't that what all the training had been for?

In her senior year, Lee Anne was advised by her many mentors to go on to graduate school. Her college adviser said it would be a crime if she didn't, and Mrs. DeHart, the high school counselor, impressed upon Ada and Buell that not only would Lee Anne be the first person on both sides of her family ever to graduate from college, but she could be the first Blue Valley native to go on to Harvard. When Harvard did indeed beckon, Ada got her teeth fixed so they could go with her to help find an apartment.

That spring, Lee Anne and four of her sorority sisters took the Volvo and went to their national convention, where Lee Anne was elected to a minor national office. On the way back—it was a clear, dry day and Lee Anne was driving—the car suddenly swerved off

the Interstate, became airborne, and slammed into a bridge abut-
ment. All of the girls sustained terrible injuries; one girl had to have
five operations to rebuild her face. Lee Anne was killed instantly.

Several months after the accident, the girl who had been sitting
next to Lee Anne was well enough to come and see Buell and Ada,
who had moved back to a trailer on Elliott Creek. She brought
some of Lee Anne's things, which had been discovered in storage
at the sorority house. One of the items was Lee Anne's guitar, and
the girl remarked that late at night when everybody was in bed,
they would sometimes hear Lee Anne down in the basement, playing the guitar and singing. She never played the songs they all sang
together, but sad old melodies that sounded like bagpipes wailing,
a number of them recognizable as hymns. The girl assured Lee
Anne's parents that everybody thought they were nice songs, but
they wondered how Lee Anne happened to know them. It was
funny, the girl went on, looking curiously around the cramped
living room, how much you could share as sisters and still not
know a person. Like right before the accident, she said, they were
all talking about what they had wanted to be when they were
children, as opposed to what they were actually going to do after
college. Lee Anne didn't want to say. They all knew that she was
going to graduate school, and on to a big professional career, but
they just kept pestering her for the heck of it. Finally she said that
all she had ever wanted to do was to be the payroll clerk at a place
called Tanner Shirt. And somebody said oh get real, what kind of
an answer is that, like, that's like aspiring to work in a freeway
tollbooth. And Lee Anne said yeah, they were probably right and
anyway, she had screwed up that opportunity real good. Nobody
would let her do that now, or worse, let her just go home and help
her grandmother make dog-hair purses. At this the girls nearly died
laughing. What an incredible thing for her to say! It was while they
were laughing hysterically that the car left the highway.

Flight Out of Egypt

"Let's go to Florida," Peggy says to Rodney. It isn't the first time. Rodney belches and pushes back from the dinette table. He's in a good mood. They've just eaten his birthday dinner, which Peggy cooked herself, selecting the menu from items she serves at the Dearborn Coach House, where she works as a waitress: beef tips in *au jus* sauce, baked potato in aluminum foil, tossed salad with the house dressing, of which Peggy sneaked home a bottle.

"Why?" he asks, to tease her. Anybody would know why. It's February in Michigan and cold enough to freeze the balls off a pool table.

Peggy fingers the locket at her throat. "I've never been to Florida, have you?"

"Once when I was a kid."

"Did you like it?"

Rodney sucks a tooth. "The sand got between my toes. I'm a city boy."

Peggy brings in the bakery cake with a single candle on it. "One to grow on!" She laughs and puts the cake in front of him. Then she sings every word of "Happy Birthday" in her flat, baby voice. While she's singing, Rodney leans around her to watch the evening news on the TV in the living room. These cornball acts of hers get him.

He eats the cake part out from under the frosting, then gets down to serious business. The frosting is sweet grainy lard whipped up fluffy, which is how he likes it.

"It's not ever going to be spring," Peggy says. She's fingering that locket again and hasn't touched her cake. "As long as you're laid off, why not go?"

"I might get called back any day." Once he asked to see inside the locket, which is a hinged gold heart. It contains a faded, brownish photograph of an old-fashioned girl with her hair up. Dishwater hair, like Peggy's probably, and light eyes that give her a ghosty, staring look. Peggy claims the picture was already in the locket when she got it. The most interesting thing about the picture is that the girl in it is actually wearing the locket. That's why Rodney remembers her and why every time Peggy touches the locket, he sees the girl's face.

"Arlene and Bob drove straight through and was in Fort Myers in twenty-four hours," Peggy says.

"I ain't got the bread."

"I have some money saved up."

Rodney doesn't like how much Peggy makes on tips. When big wheels from Ford's come to the Coach House, they can leave a tip you have to pick up with a forklift. They like Peggy because she's tiny and she blushes. She *is* cute, Rodney has to admit, except when she steps out of the shower. Then she looks like a little white rat. Once Chad Everett came in the Coach House and Peggy got his autograph, which she keeps in her lingerie drawer. In fact, Rodney hates everything about the Dearborn Coach House.

"Forget Florida," he says.

That's the end of it. Peggy gives Rodney his presents, some Jovan men's cologne and a hand-painted duck decoy to go on top of the TV; and they finish the bottle of Riunite.

But that night after Peggy goes to work and Rodney is watching TV, he starts thinking. They've been together nearly five months and this is the only thing she's ever asked for. She won't even use a piece of dental floss if he bought it. Which is more than he can say for Joanne, the last one.

He met Peggy one Sunday last spring, the morning after he'd had a night to remember up in Highland Park. He gets out of bed to answer a knock at the door, his head going like a jackhammer.

This little frizzy blond's standing there in cutoffs and a torn T-shirt, barefoot. No bra either, but anyway, she's flat.

"Is this yours?" she asks.

He takes the wallet, remembering he's seen her in the clubhouse of the apartment complex once or twice. It's his, all right, money gone.

"Where'd you find it?"

"In the dumpster, with all this." She drags over a laundry basket of bowling stuff, towels, personal papers. Some of it is messed up pretty bad. He recognizes it as the junk he's accumulated in Joanne's car, which he was driving last night. The hangover turns his stomach upside down, so he thanks Peggy fast. On the bathroom mirror Joanne has left a message in lipstick: *So long, asshole.*

After that he starts noticing Peggy standing at the bus stop on Beech Daly. One day he gives her a ride and things speed up from there. She's not exactly interesting but there are a lot of funny little things about her, like being the only adult under eighty he's ever met in Detroit who can't drive a car. Also, once they saw a possum killed on the highway and she started crying. And there's her voice. Sometimes when she's telling what happened at work, her voice makes him think of a shiny spatula sliding under one pancake after another and tossing them high in the air. The pancakes do these lazy flips, curling in on themselves and getting flatter and paler as they fall.

He talks Peggy into moving in with him, at first mostly to have someone to share the rent, but also because she seems so sweet and eager to please. Joanne was more exciting, Lorraine was prettier, and Karyn was funnier, but Peggy is the gentlest. It's after she moves in that he discovers she washes all her clothes by hand, because she doesn't know how to use a laundromat. When he makes fun of her, she starts that crying and says her family was too poor to go to the laundromat. This also explains why at first she's afraid to use the electric can opener or his blow dryer. The dead giveaway comes about a month after they've been living together. Rodney comes home in the middle of the day to get his checkbook and Peggy hasn't gone to work yet. Her teeth and gums are brown and she smells funny. The can of snuff is right out on the coffee table. She gets real upset and won't tell him where she learned to dip. The only woman he's ever heard of who does this is the great-grandmother of a man he used to work with over in Hamtramck. The guy was an Appalachian mountaineer and had brought the old woman to live with his family after she got too feeble to live alone in the hills. Rodney doesn't much care where his women come from or where they go after they leave him. If Peggy doesn't want to talk about being a Briarhopper, it's okay with him. He never catches her dipping snuff again. Anyway, he likes teaching her about all these things she never had; and just lately, he's begun to feel that he might even be lucky to have found her.

Thinking about the way she looked when he caught her with the snuff—like a little kid that's wet her pants—makes him feel bad about how he's lied to her. He's been to Florida lots of times, though always in the summer, and was even planning another trip in June. It's one of the big things he does. People he meets on the stairs in the complex are always saying, "Hey, going to Florida this year?" It's a wonder Peggy hasn't heard one of them ask him.

During a commercial, he goes to stand in front of the picture window that looks into the thick of the Sherwood Forest apartment complex. The gray snow crust on the lawn is two months old and the wind is driving flat across his vision, west to east. This is his thirty-fifth winter and the first one that's ever bothered him. He heaves a sigh and his belt buckle cuts sharply into his gut. His next pair of jeans will have to be the full-cut type for the mature man, the kind he used to kid the older guys at work about. He doesn't like giving in to women. That's why he lied to Peggy. But now he has an urge to do something unpredictable.

Three days later they wheel out of the icebound parking lot with summer clothes in their suitcases. Peggy has bought a Rand McNally road atlas and she traces routes on it with an index finger, her eyes bright and jerky like a parakeet's.

Rodney's pretty excited himself. When they turn south on Telegraph Road he yells, "All ri-ight!" and flips on the radio full blast.

They're nearly to Monroe, on I–75, when Peggy makes a noise.

"Say what?"

"It's that land along the highway," she says. "The strips of grass in the middle and along the shoulder. There's a lot of ground like that downtown too, like between the street and the sidewalk, sometimes with a pitiful little tree on it. It gives me the creeps."

"Yeah?"

"It doesn't belong to anybody. Don't you see? Looking at that grass makes me want to cry. I wish it was artificial."

He pushes in the car lighter.

"Land should belong to somebody, to a family or a person." Peggy's voice is loud, and flatter than ever. "I hate it like it is in Detroit. It isn't land anymore."

Rodney switches channels to catch the news. Peggy's not what he would call smart, but sometimes she's hard to understand.

The minute they leave Wayne County, she shuts up the maps and goes to sleep.

Two hours later, he wakes her for a pit stop. "You're missing the whole trip. I thought you wanted to see something different."

"It isn't different yet."

She's asleep again in two minutes. As he drives, Rodney eats the sandwiches she packed. He's started to pick up a Golden Oldies station outside Cincinnati and between bites he sings along with Tommy Edwards on "It's All in the Game" and with Bobby Vinton, his all-time favorite, on "Red Roses for a Blue Lady."

Going over the bridge from Cincinnati to Covington, Kentucky, Peggy wakes up.

"Look! The Ohio River!" She bounces up and down like a little kid.

"It's not that big." He's looking around for Riverfront Stadium, where the Reds play.

"But the *Ohio*."

"The Detroit River's bigger."

"The Detroit River's like that grass that nobody owns," she says.

The minute the wheels touch Kentucky, she says, "Pull over. Anywhere."

Thinking she's carsick, he does it.

She gets out and walks off the shoulder into the weeds. Her back is to him but he can tell she's holding the locket at her throat, stroking it. She reminds him of women praying in the Catholic church where his mother goes.

When she returns he asks, "What was that all about?"

"I was making a wish." She pats his knee and looks away. "You're good to me, Rodney. Thanks."

Maybe it's that time of the month, he puzzles. Sometimes she gets kind of weird just before.

She sleeps all the way to Lexington, but only catnapping now, waking abruptly to look around her. Rodney doesn't mind. He's not much of a talker, especially to women. He passes the time thinking about the summer he drove an eighteen-wheeler for his uncle, which is what he should have stuck with. It was the best time of his life, but it's too late to go back to it now.

At Lexington it's around dinnertime, so he exits and drives in toward the city until he finds a Hardee's. He's surprised when Peggy has another idea.

"Can we go over there?" She points at a converted frame house with a red neon sign, Dixie Kitchen. The paint is peeling. It's out of place on franchise row.

He orders a Dixieburger and fries. She gets soup beans and cornbread.

"Where'd you learn that? Go to school with some of those Kentucky Briarhoppers?" Rodney asks.

She bites into a Saltine. Her nose moves like a rabbit's. "I knew some."

Rodney snorts a laugh. "Briars! There were a lot of them in Hamtramck where I worked. All they could think about was making enough to go back to their little chickenshit farms in the hills, where they left their families. They sent money back every month, like Mexicans or something. They didn't know nothing from nothing. It was like they were from a different planet." It's pretty funny watching Peggy's face. Serves her right for thinking that she can fool an old fooler like him.

After dinner he says, "Why don't we just spend the night here? I'm getting a backache."

"Just another hour," she begs. "Think of those warm beaches."

Following her directions, they somehow get turned around and miss getting back on the Interstate. Peggy takes the flashlight out of the glove compartment and studies the Rand McNally, chewing her lip and stroking the locket with her thumb. "It's all right. We can take a shortcut and link back up with the Interstate another way."

Half an hour later they're out of Lexington all right, way the hell out in pitch-black countryside. There's a wild and desolate feel to things. The way the headlights hit the two-lane blacktop makes Rodney think of every sad country song he's ever heard.

"This is wrong. Turn on the overhead light. Lemme see the map," he says.

Peggy starts snuffling. "You think I'm stupid. You've always thought so."

"Let me see the goddamned map. Florida's the other way."

"Please, honey," she's really crying now, "I can set us right. You just think because I can't handle some things back home. . . ." She breaks down entirely.

Women, he thinks. "All right. But you better know what you're doing."

"I do. You'll see," she whispers tearily.

Another thirty miles and they see neon ahead.

"Here," Peggy says.

It's the Southern Belle Motel and Restaurant, twenty-two units, steam heat, free TV, and vacancy.

The old man behind the desk looks like something out of "Hee Haw."

He gives them a long, calculating stare. "All the rooms have twin beds."

"That'll be fine," Peggy says.

Rodney eyes her but he doesn't say anything. Anyway, he can't believe how cheap the room is.

Peggy changes in the bathroom, climbs into bed, and curls up in a ball right in the middle, like she's afraid something's going to get her feet.

Rodney's lying on the other bed, watching "Hill Street Blues." There's a lot of snow on the screen.

Peggy's head is under the covers. In a muffled voice she asks, "Can we drive around tomorrow before we leave?"

"Here? Why?"

"There's a town on the map."

"What's to see?"

"Please, Rodney. You said you wanted to get away from Detroit. This is real different."

"How do you know?"

"It's the South. It has to be. Please."

"What the hell's going on? Ever since you got the idea of going to Florida, you think you're running the whole show. You forget who wears the pants?" he grouses.

"No."

"Then what the hell are you doing over in that bed?"

The mound of covers breathes up and down, up and down. All at once she sits up. Her face is pink, her nose sharp: the white rat look.

"If I come over there, can we drive around tomorrow?"

"I'll think about it. Come here."

In the night he wakes up and she's not beside him. He can just make out her silhouette against the window. She's drawn the drapes all the way back and there are a lot of stars. She's swaying in front of them as if she's listening to a song he can't hear.

At dawn she shakes him awake. She's dressed and packed.

"Come on. Let's get going," she says, bouncing on the balls of her feet.

He isn't going anywhere without two cups of coffee and a cigarette. They're the only people in the restaurant. Peggy drinks a glass of water.

In the car he follows the signs to Douthit, "a friendly little place to stop, pop. 528," until Peggy points off to the right, toward some blue hills. Rodney sees a dirt road cutting up the hill, past a faded red barn with SEE ROCK CITY painted on the side.

"That way."

"By God, Peggy, you've been here before!" he yells.

She hunches away from him.

"Where're we going? You answer me!"

"I just want to see something." She keeps her face turned to the window.

"You know somebody around here?"

"It won't take long. I swear." Her voice sounds like a flat rock skipping over water.

He makes the turn. "Think you're so damned smart. You never fooled me. Not for a minute."

"I didn't?"

"Hell, no. So you're a Briar. Big deal. Look, I would have taken you here without all this sneaking around, if you'd asked." His face gets hot. He probably would have. And he doesn't go out of his way for anybody.

Almost immediately, the road gets hilly and winding, with tricky hairpin turns. Pretty soon it's down to two wheel ruts. Weeds brush the underside of the car like fingers reaching to slow them down. The banks on either side of the road are damp, yellowish clay. Rodney watches for road signs, houses, even a hunting poster to give him a clue. There's nothing. The forest closes in.

"What is this, a damn Indian trail? How much farther?"

Peggy doesn't answer. She's sitting forward, hands gripping the top of her purse. Her lips twitch a couple of times, as if she's talking to somebody in her head. Her eyes are wide and still. Looking at her from the side, he can see right through the pale blue bulge of the irises, as if they're glass eyes in a doll. The hair on the back of his neck prickles.

"Hey. What building did you live in at Sherwood Forest before you moved in with me?"

"I don't remember the number. You know which one."

"No, I don't know. We always went to my place. You always said your roommate was asleep in the living room. I used to let you off at the clubhouse."

"What?" She's squinting ahead.

"When you moved in, you brought your stuff over while I was at work. You know what I think, Peggy? I don't think you even lived in Sherwood For—"

"Watch out!" she shrieks.

The thing in the middle of the road is stringy-limbed, brown, red-eyed. Rodney slews the wheel to the left and there's a sickening sound of ripping metal underneath them. The exhaust suddenly gets much louder. When he looks again, the creature is gone.

"Wild boar," Peggy breathes.

He guns the motor, then tries shifting gears to rock the car. No luck.

They get out. The muffler is lying several yards back. Rodney squats down, trying to get a look underneath. "Get me the jack."

He kneels, cursing, getting muddy. The big vein in his temple starts thudding. "We'll need a bulldozer to get out of this clay."

He stands up and kicks a wheel. "What the hell're you doing back there?" He stamps around to the trunk. It's open. The jack is lying there in plain sight. He looks around him. This is the quietest place he's ever been. "Peggy?" The catches on the suitcase he loaned her are sprung. The suitcase is empty.

By now it's around nine and weak February sunlight is dripping through the trees. Rodney zips up his jacket and starts walking. He can't believe he's putting up with this. Except for where the car mired down, the ground is too rocky to hold a footprint; but there's no other way for her to have gone. Within five minutes the two ruts have dwindled to one narrow path. He trudges on, yelling her name once in a while and wishing he had the pack of cigarettes back on the dashboard. He kicks the ice skim off the puddles. He's been too easy on Peggy all along, he realizes. He's spoiled her. But that's going to change, as soon as he gets hold of her again.

The path bends through a ravine, hugging an outcropping of limestone on one side, with a sheer drop on the other down to a creek. Then the woods open up and he's on the edge of a clearing. Ahead is a long log house with a rough stone chimney. To one side is a well with a bucket on a pulley rigged up over it. A couple of weathered outbuildings stand back against the side of the hill. Something doesn't look right. After a minute he gets it. There are no power lines running to the house. But what's weirder, the tree by the porch has apples on it. In February. He looks around the clearing again. The grass is summer green. It's a lot hotter and brighter here than it was back on the path.

He walks toward the house through a heavy, ticking silence, which his feet explode when they hit the porch steps. The porch columns are tree trunks with the bark left on. Before knocking on the door, he looks in a window.

The inside is one big room, with a ladder leading to a loft. Two women are sitting at a table with their backs to him, peeling vegetables. A man sits on a straight chair by the fireplace, cleaning an old-type gun. One of the women is heavy and soft, with gray hair done up in a bun. The other one is younger and little, no bigger than a minute, with hair the same way. Both are in old-timey clothes.

The man's a tall, rawboned character with a bushy black beard and black hair combed in slick strands across his forehead.

Rodney knocks on the door, leaning to keep looking in the window. The three people inside go on with their tasks. He pounds on the door again, yelling for Peggy. Even deaf people would feel the vibrations, but they don't. While he's pounding a third time, he notices that the door has leather hinges. His chest tightens like he's going to have a coronary.

Just as he goes back to the window, the young woman puts down the potato she's peeling and goes over to the kettle hanging over the fire. When Rodney sees her face, his mind twists like a kaleidoscope making one design out of another. It's the face of the woman in the locket. But it's Peggy's face too. That is, it's Peggy in a different way of life in another time. As she leans to lift the cover off, the locket swings free of her collar and catches the light.

He can't find the path out of there, though he knows exactly where it should be, so he ends up plunging down the hillside, falling, sliding on his butt, scrambling up, tearing his jacket on branches, twisting an ankle when he loosens a rock slide. It's freezing and his breath rasps like a hacksaw blade in his throat as he keeps going down, crossing another creek, losing track of time. When he finally stops, all done in, a faint, familiar roar comes to him. He staggers over one more rise and breaks through a thicket, and there's the damned Interstate, rolling along like gangbusters.

He hitches into Douthit and tells his story at the Mountain View Cafe, but nobody believes him, because there hasn't been a road up Boar Hollow since the loggers left fifty years ago. He makes so much noise that a deputy sheriff finally drives him out to the SEE ROCK CITY barn to prove it to him. Sure enough, there's an unbroken fence where he thought the road was. His car is in the ditch next to it with the muffler torn off.

Back in town while he's waiting for his car to be fixed, Rodney hears the deputy say something over the phone about maybe searching the Michigan car for funny cigarettes and maybe finding some, if they need more time to check out the missing woman angle. Rodney pays cash for the repair work and gets out of town fast.

In Detroit he tries to forget what happened. There's nothing else to do. Sometimes when he's drinking, he can convince himself that he had some type of hallucination on the road during an argument with Peggy, a delayed reaction to some drugs he did years back. That way she becomes just one more woman who cut out on him before he did the same to her. But other times when he sees a big eighteen-wheeler on the freeway, his mind will go bizarre on him and he'll wonder things. Like, how long had she been looking for a way to get home and why couldn't she just hop a bus? Maybe, he'll decide, it had to be a person. She had to find a person willing to take her. Like a union rule or something. But why him? He goes over the first couple of times he spoke to her and remembers that he was kind to her, more or less. Kinder than he usually is with women, because she wasn't his physical type and so he wasn't thinking of making her. And when he thinks that he, Rodney, might have been the kindest person she ever ran into, he'll be swept by a feeling so empty that he wants to cry. Then he knows it all really happened.

It's begun to worry him how many eighteen-wheelers there are in Motor City.

Small Caucasian Woman

We keep up on things fairly well out here, even though our only neighbors are cows. Whoever built this facility must have supposed that old people need the kind of peace and quiet you can only get in a field three miles from town; as if we won't have all the peace and quiet we can handle, soon enough. But somebody's got a radio or television on all the time and we get the local newspaper after the staff finishes with it. Every so often one of us gets sprung for dinner with our children. And we pick up news not meant for us: it's surprising how many people will assume that if you're wearing a hearing aid, you can't hear anything. The trouble is, it's hard to care about any of it when you've been cleaned up and set on a shelf to wait for Uncle Death to take you for a Sunday drive. So what happens in town these days is just another soap opera to watch. Or was, until May Linda.

Like most small towns, Blue Valley is a place where things used to happen. In this one they talk about the feuds early in the century that bullet-pocked the courthouse; the 1939 flood that caught a circus on the fairgrounds and washed pythons and monkeys up Slate Creek; the 1946 state high school basketball championship. The last big event was the Interstate bypassing us twenty-five years ago. The sense that everything has already happened has led many citizens to feel that they have a great deal to protect and preserve here. To them, out of the want ads of the *Blue Valley News* that Wednesday morning in April, hissed the Serpent.

> Small Caucasian woman desires gentleman
> for mature relationship. Nine-year-old
> boy included.

42

In its ninety-eight years of operation, the *News* had never printed a personal ad before, there being no need to advertise one's private affairs in a town small enough for everyone already to know them. Moreover, to ask publicly for help in satisfying any need more intimate than selling a used backhoe or giving away free kittens went against the gnarled and ingrown independence of our hill ways. We suspected a city type, or at least someone from outside the region, set down by chance, like a spore carried in on the wind. The next Sunday one of our young ministers thundered for two hours against the corruption of the fabric of our nation by a foreign power, until an elder of the congregation whispered to him that Caucasian meant white and possibly Anglo-Saxon. In Blue Valley these are congruent sets, taking in every single inhabitant. But the idea of foreignness took hold, encouraged by the newspaper editor's pious refusal to pull the ad, in defense of the First Amendment and rapidly increasing circulation. So the rumors continued to crossbreed until the Mafia was operating out of the Planet Motel up on the Interstate, poised to take over the IGA Foodliner.

Then a bottle was thrown on Railroad Street.

Once the brash, honky-tonk entertainment district, Railroad Street is today four dusty blocks of weed-choked lots and empty storefronts along the abandoned tracks at the bottom of town. Sometime in the fifties, helped along by another defeat of the liquor referendum due to an alliance of the church and bootlegger interests, it died of our respectability. No one thinks about it or goes there, though at night its lingering aura of illicit pleasures floats unrecognized into many a dream.

That particular Saturday evening, a prosperous farmer and his wife, after spending the evening in town visiting relatives, took a wrong turn and found themselves driving down Railroad Street. Just opposite the decaying freight station, an object hit their car. They braked, looked around. Later the woman said that it was as if, crossing a graveyard at night, they had found themselves suddenly surrounded by spirits. The dead street was alive, its telltale heart two lighted windows over the boarded-up junk store. Shadows flickered across the cracked shades; radio music and voices spilled down. Cigarettes glowed in the recessed entrance to the junk store and several cars hugged the curb in front of it. Under the next streetlight they passed a late-model sports car with its engine running. As her husband slowed to turn the corner back toward civilization, the woman glimpsed inside the vehicle the white, black-lettered fronts of several high school team jackets.

The farmer and his wife drove straight to the police station, from whence they telephoned their oldest son, a perennial winner in the school board elections on the strength of his having been a starting forward on the 1946 championship team. Within the hour, the chief of police was forced to take action on knowledge that he and the girls at the telephone office had shared for days: the phone number listed in the small Caucasian woman's ad belonged to the rented room above the Railroad Street junk store. The sleeping dragon of that thoroughfare had raised its head again, its yellow eyes slanting with evil, its talons curved to rake in our athletes, keeping them out past curfew and ruining their chances of going to the regionals.

By the time we heard that she had been jailed overnight, a black-rooted blond with an unpronounceable foreign surname, she was on her way out of town. From the nursing home we saw the police car go by on its way to drop her at the gas station off the Interstate access ramp. She had been no trouble to the jailer, except to ask for Kotex when he brought her breakfast; whereupon he, a man of legendary ignorance, had replied that she could eat cornflakes or nothing.

The afternoon shift, arriving at three, brought more of the story. She had listed her occupation as exotic dancer and her age as twenty-seven. She had refused to reveal the whereabouts of the nine-year-old boy. She had insisted, through hours of questioning, that her advertisement was sincere, that she only wanted one permanent companion, the last man, she hoped, with whom she would ever have to deal. She was saddened and bewildered that the people of her hometown would think otherwise. And this was the kicker, of course: that she was no foreign contaminant at all, no stray bit of urban blight, but, underneath her extra surname, merely a McFann.

Into the hundreds of years of local history we shared, we reached back to that vanished breed of welfare cases, unimaginative criminals, and petty evangelists that had once infested the entire county. No one could say when the last one had disappeared or if in fact there were a few, inexplicably spared by the process of natural selection, that still lived here. They were less than nothing to the town; yet one of them at least, this May Linda McFann, thought of Blue Valley as home, just as we did. That gave us pause. Home is generally the place a person has been the happiest.

Toward evening, we saw her for the first time.

She was wobbling along the road on impossibly high heels, wearing jeans and a balding velveteen jacket: a pale, chihuahua-boned woman on the far side of thirty-five. The thin black crescent of an old shiner hung under one eye. In some of us, the sight of her triggered a memory: that of a small, dishwater-colored shadow that used to flit around old Jakeleg McFann as he sat in his wheelchair in front of the bus station, selling the same five yellow pencils for thirty years and repulsing with scorn the occasional stranger who actually tried to buy one. This woman, then, who had walked seven miles in order to pass us and who had another three to go before she reached town again, was the granddaughter who had brought Jake his lunch packed in a coffee can, on her school lunch hour, and who had taken him back to his rented room at night. Others remembered her later in life, as a sallow, ponytailed teenager who, when one of her brothers was being taken to trial for chewing a man's ear off in a fight, had slipped through the escorting officers to press into his manacled hands a Milky Way bar. Sometime after that, as typically happened to McFann girls, she had "gone bad" and left town.

The next day we heard how Police Chief Watson had intercepted her about eight o'clock in the evening, as she toiled up Main Street carrying the now broken-down high heels. When he threatened to run her out of town again, for the first and only time she spoke up, and loudly enough for several loiterers to hear, saying that if anyone had outraged decency, it was the several prominent citizens, whose names she would be pleased to mention then and there, who had answered her honest proposition with other propositions that made even her blush, to say nothing of how such ideas might affect their wives.

She found work at the lunch counter in the bus station. The boy, oddly soft and pale and quick, like a newt, turned up in Miss Aggie Carr's third-grade class. May Linda renewed the newspaper ad for a week; but now that the word was out about her lack of confidentiality, interest died. Railroad Street relapsed into somnolence. The town swiveled its attention to the alcoholic breakdown of the president of the Women's Club.

Thus nobody was on alert the afternoon a wiry, white-haired man in faded overalls sat down at May Linda's counter and told her a story. He introduced himself as Bert Cornett, a retired coal miner living in the Maple Shade community some fifteen miles into the hills northeast of Blue Valley. Due to black lung disease from his years in the mines, he had been on disability for some time; but he was getting along fine until his old woman died, a year and a half before. During fifty-one years of marriage and the rearing of five children, he had never given one thought to her preceding him in death, since he daily expected to be carried off by a mine accident or pneumonia. Her demise knocked the sense out of him; so that it was not until nearly six weeks after the funeral that he came to himself and realized that he was still sleeping on the living room couch while some of his funeral guests—his daughter Junie, her ne'er-do-well husband, Ralph, and their indeterminate number of children—occupied the two bedrooms of the four-room house. The first pension check he cashed, Junie took for groceries. That seemed reasonable to him, since he had neglected to buy food toward the end of his wife's illness. But when he refused to hand over the money a second time, his daughter knocked him to the kitchen floor, pinned him with a chair, and took it. He must have forgotten, she screeched, that Ralph was unable to work because he was nervous and she had to stay at home for her children (all of whom were away from six-thirty in the morning until the school bus brought them back at four). Therefore, Bert's pension belonged to everybody, an old son-of-a-bitch like himself being lucky to have family around him in his old age.

Here he lifted his forelock to reveal a three-inch gash, the result of Junie's pushing him off the back porch the week before, when he had demanded money for chewing tobacco; and he added that twice he had been locked out of the house all night for arguing politics with his son-in-law.

He rummaged in his pockets and took out several items one at a time, explaining each as he laid it on the counter. The scrap of

newsprint was May Linda's want ad; the photograph of his wife in
her coffin proved he was a widower; the wedding ring, hers, could
be May Linda's now; the ten-dollar bill and the three ones, he had
had to steal back from Junie that morning before catching a ride
into town with the Wonder Bread man; the pension papers and the
deed to the shack constituted his estate. After he died, May Linda
could have the pocket watch and the penknife too. In return for all
these things, he asked for a quiet place to live out his days at his
own pace, for her not to tell Junie where he was, and for a little
tobacco money. Tobacco, he explained, gave him pep.

All this time May Linda had been wiping the counter from one
end to the other and back again, her eyes lowered on her task. Now
she poured a glass of water and gave it to Bert, who had begun to
wheeze. He could have all the tobacco he wanted, she said, but she
didn't care about the pep. She had experienced enough pep from
men to last her for the rest of her life. What she wanted was a good
man to set an example for her boy and a place to rest. A place to
rest meant a place or a thing she wouldn't have to leave, and that
wouldn't leave her. Bert said that he understood. But, May Linda
warned him, there might be some little trouble about getting married. She might still have a husband, though she wouldn't know
where to find him. However, since the ceremony had been Catholic, she thought it might not count. Some of it hadn't even been in
English. She promised to find out. Bert said there wasn't any hurry.
He'd rather live in sin than be beaten to death by his own daughter
in a state of grace.

When the boy straggled in from school, she fed both of them
supper at the end of the counter, paying for the meals out of her tips
for the week. At the end of her shift, they went home together to
Railroad Street.

But we did not know any of this yet. Summer passed to fall to
winter without us knowing, during which time May Linda must have
lived and worked in plain sight yet with increasing invisibility, gradually resuming her identity as one of the interchangeable McFanns, a
background figure as unremarked upon as a crack in the sidewalk,
someone who might, after all, have been residing here since childhood, for all anyone could be sure. Bert, who stayed inside to keep
the cold air from needling his lungs, did not yet exist for us.

Around Christmas we first heard about the elderly amnesia patient from the aides, talking among themselves. He was in the convalescent wing, often on oxygen, having been transferred from the county hospital with nothing but his hospital gown. A month earlier he had been found lying in front of the emergency room doors, filthy, malnourished, and delirious. The only word he had said in the hospital was *bastards,* repeated several times. But since then, he had told a social worker that although he recognized nothing of Blue Valley, he did remember a strong smell of ocean, wearing a yellow slicker, and a word he couldn't precisely recall but that sounded Indian. These details sent them looking for him, or rather for the lack of him, on the Atlantic coast.

Early in the new year he was well enough to join our general population. We would see him in his wheelchair in the community room, oblivious to all activity, gray and limp as a pile of soiled laundry. But Sadie Novak, something of a malingerer herself, did not believe in amnesia. She set herself to get to know him, rolling her wheelchair next to his nearly every day after breakfast.

It took a long time to break through, because Bert Cornett was scared. But in bits and pieces, talking when he was certain no staff was listening, he told how he and May Linda and the boy, Sammy, had met and how they had lived together: how at night while she soaked her feet, she would talk about Detroit and he would tell a little about the mines; how she would shave him every Sunday morning while they listened to church on the radio; and how the boy would be playing on the floor with toy cars and asking questions. In those evenings Bert told May Linda how he and his old woman had dreamed of moving to Arizona where he could breathe better and her arthritis wouldn't act up so much. They had planned every detail, what they would take in only two suitcases and how they would bind themselves up with cheese for the long bus trip; but all along they had known it was just a game, like imagining what they would buy from the Montgomery Ward catalog if they were millionaires. Directly, May Linda said maybe they ought to try Bert's dream for real, since the dream that had kept her going in Detroit, of living as a respectable citizen in Blue Valley, wasn't turning out too well. She began to put away part of his pension money for the trip.

Finally Bert told about the morning that he was home alone as usual, breathing better because of some new medicine but still only able to listen to the radio and watch over the pot of soup beans cooking for supper. He was making a buzzer toy for the boy out of a button and a piece of string, when a horn blew downstairs. The borrowed car held Junie, Ralph, and a middle daughter, little Annette. Annette was the only one of his grandchildren he cared about or who cared about him, a sickly child who would listen to the stories of his boyhood and who preferred reading, sometimes to him, to torturing small animals with her siblings. When she rolled down the window, calling *Grandpa Grandpa,* and he saw that she had been crying, he went down to the street to see her, his only thought to give her the buzzer toy and to make a new one for the boy.

Junie was as sweet as pie to him, not saying a word about how he had gone out to the mailbox back in May and had never returned. She handed him a box of his favorite store-bought cookies, asked if she might use the bathroom, and suggested he have a seat in the back with Annette and hear the child's multiplication tables while she went upstairs. Even after she came back and Ralph pulled away from the curb with the news that they were going to see Bud, Bert's son in Sawville who had come home once in the last fifteen years, to spend forty-five minutes at his mother's funeral, even then it took Bert ten miles to realize he had been kidnapped. And still he did not suspect why Junie had gone upstairs until, in Bud's driveway, she waved the deed and pension papers under his nose. As soon as he signed over everything to her and Bud he could go back to his harlot, she said, if he was stupid enough to think the woman would take him back dead-broke. She cursed him for a lecherous old fool and a disgrace to the family. And he was a fool, Bert told Sadie Novak, or he would never have answered that May Linda was not like a wife to him, but a daughter. For that was the remark ever after that Junie threw up to him when she hit him. He never saw Annette again.

Because Bert had his dignity, we never learned all that happened in the back bedroom of his son's house, where he eventually slid into pneumonia, pulling every breath through lungs as heavy and spongy as wet wool. But in the long afternoons with Sadie and,

gradually, others of us, he unwound the substance of those shifting, lost days, untangling dreaming from waking, truth from lies,
hearing again the voices of his own blood fuming over May Linda's
disappearance from Blue Valley with the joint bank account she
and Bert had established; their futile attempts to find and punish
her; the delicate problem of how to keep their father alive long
enough to pauperize him; and after he had signed away everything
and the pension had somehow been cashed in—for the news of
May Linda's departure had broken him—what to do with him.
Only when he hit the concrete in front of the emergency room and
lay choking in the exhaust of Bud's car was he sure that they would
stop short of murder. Now he was resolved to a life of anonymity,
believing that if he revealed his identity, the authorities would do
nothing more than notify his children, which was the last thing he
or they wanted. Let people go on looking for him elsewhere. He
barely had a claim on an identity anyway, with his money and his
house and May Linda gone.

Sadie Novak, however, was a hard-boiled romantic, a streetwise
sentimentalist. Also she had a grandniece, a shifty-eyed teenager
named Risa. Risa had been in some minor trouble with the law;
and as part of the sentence handed down in juvenile court, she was
required to spend a certain number of hours volunteering at the
nursing home. Sadie used her as a gofer whenever she could. Without telling Bert, she sent Risa to find out, as discreetly as possible,
what had become of May Linda. That suited the girl's sneakiness
fine. More subtle than any beast of the field, she nosed around
town for three days. The fourth afternoon she materialized beside
Bert's wheelchair and put something in his hand: his pocket watch,
left behind the day he was kidnapped.

One eye on the charge nurse, Risa whispered how she had picked
up May Linda's trail leading out of Blue Valley and eighteen miles
down the Interstate to the next exchange. How when she walked
in the kitchen of the franchised restaurant where May Linda was
chopping lettuce for twenty-four hours' worth of tossed salad orders, and asked if she cared to know how Bert Cornett was getting
along, May Linda put down the knife as gently as if it were an egg
and asked, *Are you his kin?* and when Risa said *No,* she let out her

breath and closed her eyes and said, *Then if you say he's alive, I'll believe you.*

She came to visit every Thursday, her day off, always with a small gift—a plastic comb, a bag of hard candy. But she pretended to be visiting someone else and only happened to talk to Bert among others. The mountaineer's suspicion of institutions, which many of us shared, ran too deep for her to behave otherwise. Besides, the mistrust had been validated when, four days after his disappearance, she had reported Bert missing. It had taken her that long to convince herself that she would not be charged with his murder; and in fact she was held overnight for questioning, finally being released for want of the murder victim or, as the country judge translated *corpus delicti,* "the corpse is delighted to be elsewhere." The pot of charred soup beans that she had presented as evidence of Bert's unpremeditated departure was still being held by the police; although Chief Watson had opined with a wink that the old codger, probably tired of trying to satisfy a woman half his age, had run for his life. Yet she had continued to sidle into the police station every day or two, to ask again that the lake be dragged and the woods be combed, since Bert got light-headed when he couldn't breathe and might simply have wandered off; until the day the sergeant told her that Bert was back with his family, and if a man was with his family, he was where he was supposed to be.

So she was at a dead end about Bert; and by now the boy had problems too serious to ignore. The fights at school were making him meaner than the Detroit streets had, because he didn't understand these fights, didn't have a clue that the very facelessness of which his mother had despaired in the city had protected them both, but that in a small town everyone is assigned a role by unspoken agreement—genius, beauty queen, patriarch, fool—and it is for life. If the town drunk does not exist, it becomes necessary to invent him. Sammy, who in the city was just a boy, was now the whore's son. To become something else, he would have to die or move away. May Linda, who had come home in search of respectability and a half-remembered happiness, had brought her son to a place where the most he could hope for was to be relegated to the substructure of society where the McFanns had always lived, part of the negative human component—the poor, the illiterate, the afflicted, the old—which by contrast defines the positive world of the powerful, the well-to-do, the complacent. Bethel, the town to which she had just moved, was too close to her origins to be any different. And we lived in her world now, having been released from our customary roles by the premature death of life in a nursing home. In a twist on the Supreme Being of the Deists, we had created the town and its inhabitants—our descendants—and then were banished to the outer edge of its universe: not by our own indifference, but by the indifference of our creations to us. Omniscient and impotent, we were waiting for the ultimate relocation, bragging about our important grandchildren who never came to see us. Bert had a chance at something else, Sadie reminded us, but he needed help.

We picked a Sunday morning, when nearly everyone was at the nondenominational service in the community room. Bert stayed in his room. The rest of us took our stations. At precisely eleven forty-five, as he always did, the minister brought his sermon to a close and signaled to Mrs. Cotter at the piano, who launched into "Leaning on the Everlasting Arms." Under cover of the music we heard the growl of a powerful automobile crawling around the circle drive in front. Bert came out of his room at the far end of the hall, wearing a red bow tie and fresh overalls and carrying a paper sack of belongings. At first it looked easy; but gradually time and distance, never dependable here, tilted out of whack. The farther Bert came in his uncertain shuffle, the more the hall lengthened and inclined, until he seemed to be struggling in slow motion up a long glass hill. Sadie Novak, positioned in her wheelchair by the front doors, motioned encouragement to him. When he was a third of the way along, an aide wandered out of the lounge and, seeing Bert dressed differently from an hour before, asked where he was going. But by prearrangement, one-hundred-and-one-year-old Chester Martin called out in pain, deflecting the aide into his room. Bert was within twenty feet of the doors when the charge nurse came out of the east wing and saw what waited at the front steps: a shiny black stock car with the rear end jacked up and orange flames painted down the sides. In the back seat, stiff as tintypes, sat May Linda and her son. Sadie's grandniece Risa sat in front with a man roughly the size and hairiness of a Kodiak bear. The charge nurse took one look at the car, one at Bert, and screamed for the orderlies, as her entire future salary passed before her eyes. Two of them came barreling out of the community room, where the hymn was dissolving in confusion as other residents became aware of the disturbance. Just as the first orderly caught up with Bert, Sadie's hand came out from under her lap robe, holding what looked to be a small pistol. When the orderly laughed that he had seen those little pistol-shaped cigarette lighters before, Sadie put two bullets in the ceiling. The second orderly, who had bulled through the door ahead of Bert, found himself confronting the driver of the car, who smiled peaceably down at the lad while adjusting his studded leather wristbands. With a wave to us, Bert tottered to the car.

The same authorities who had been unable to connect the disappearance of an infirm, seventy-year-old man with the subsequent appearance of a seventy-year-old amnesiac in the same town, told us within hours that Bert and May Linda and the boy had been seen boarding a Greyhound bus in Lexington. From the little family itself, we did not hear for years, until May Linda finally wrote from Scottsdale, Arizona, to tell us how happy Bert had been for the last two and a half years of his life. She had meant to write sooner, she apologized to the addressee, but most of their savings had gone into establishing their new life and it had taken much longer than she expected to save the enclosed.

Although we were no longer living in Blue Valley, Blue Valley still lived in us; so that it was not until after the five-hundred-dollar check did not bounce and we had bought with it the television set for the community room bearing the plaque she had requested, *In Memory of Bert Cornett,* that we finally, completely, believed in her.

Blanche Long Tells What Keeps Shug Watson Going

If you're a regular shopper at the IGA, sooner or later you'll run into Shug Watson and you'll see what I mean about her. With her husband, Bill Tom, so bad now, the grocery and the beauty parlor are about the only places Shug goes. If she's gone from the house for more than a couple of hours, Bill Tom gets scared and then when she gets home he'll be a lot sicker, maybe even bad enough that Shug will have to take him to Emergency. He's been that way for three years. They have over $20,000 in medical bills and no particular way to pay.

If somebody would pay Shug by the hour for the work she does, they would have paid off that bill a long time ago. She and her brother Sonny were raised on a farm up around Sockleg and she still keeps farmer's hours. Many a morning she'll be at the grocery store by seven-thirty, having already bathed, dressed, and fed Bill Tom; baked two pies and put a roast in the oven; done three loads of laundry; and waxed the kitchen floor. When Shug was ten, her mother died and she took over the housekeeping for Sonny and the old man. That's where she learned to work like a pack mule, canning all their vegetables, milking, chopping firewood, and doing the clothes in one of those old wringer washers. She looks, however, with her painted-on jeans, soft curvy sweaters, prancing filly walk, and milk-and-honey skin and hair, like she never lifted anything heavier than a hairbrush. She is always smiling.

Her brother Sonny didn't like to work so well. One day when he was sixteen and Shug was thirteen, she asked him to pick some beans for supper and he said he would right after he went in the house to do something. The next they heard from him was three months later, when the State Police out in Oregon called to say they had arrested him for shoplifting. He gave them the slip before they could send him home. Right after Sonny left, Old Man Maxwell married a widow woman with three children and Shug had all of them to do for.

She has a pleasant voice, low and trembly, and she used to sing in a gospel quartet at her church. At the Big Sing over at Willow Chapel she met Bill Tom, who sang bass with a group from town. They were married a couple of weeks later; she was fifteen and he was twenty. He called her Skeeter because she was so tiny compared to him.

By the time Shug was eighteen she had the two boys and Jeanette and was working full-time at the Dairy Bar. Bill Tom was the best old thing but he drove a truck and was gone a lot. Like in the song, it was wake me up early, be good to my dogs, and teach my children to pray; and off he went. Then the mill burned and he lost his job. Shug had to work double shifts at the Dairy Bar while Bill Tom brooded at home, imagining her flirting with the customers. She never did; he was always the only one for her. But there were terrible scenes if she was even fifteen minutes late getting home. They might not have stayed together if their oldest son hadn't caught spinal meningitis when he was seven and died overnight. That bound them together again.

After Junior's death Shug had two miscarriages and then another boy, Eldon. Meanwhile her daddy passed away. The stepchildren scattered and her stepmother came down with Alzheimer's disease—Shug always pronounces it Old Timer's disease—so she brought the stepmother to live with them and cared for her till the end. During this time she also took in sewing and baked pies for people. Bill Tom was working again, but there was never enough money. Pretty soon her own children were getting married and divorced. There were grandchildren being left alone all day to take care of themselves, so Shug took them in. She completely raised one grandson from the age of two until he went in the army. Next month she'll be a great-grandmother and no doubt will get the privilege of toilet training that one too. Fortunately for everybody else, Shug has always stayed healthy, except for the mastectomy.

Knowing all of this, anybody would wonder how she can look not a day over thirty-five when she is actually fifty-two, how anybody that looks like she would break a bone if she sneezed can be so durable. She actually looks younger than her daughter Jeanette, which is ironic because Jeanette is the secret of Shug's youth and serene acceptance of things.

Shug never exactly slighted her boys; but she left their development up to their father. Boys will make their own way or the world will make it for them, she always said. Jeanette, meantime, had the prettiest bedroom that could be ordered by mail, all pink satin and white French provincial with gold trim. Shug saw that she had piano lessons, baton lessons, dancing and singing lessons. Though she herself could barely read and write, she stood over Jeanette every night until the homework was done, so that Jeanette nearly always made the B honor roll in high school. The studying paid off in a big way. When Jeanette was seventeen, she entered the county Junior Miss pageant, singing "Peace in the Valley" for her talent. At the end of the competition she was tied with one of the Whittaker girls, who had had many more advantages, until the emcee asked the tiebreaker question, "What word does r-a-t-h-o-l-e spell?" That's when the studying paid off.

The minute Jeanette won the contest, Shug called her brother Sonny and began to make arrangements. Sonny had stayed out West and was doing all right for himself, running a crap table in Las Vegas. Shug thought he could help Jeanette find a career in entertainment. Before she got her way, she had the biggest fight of her life with Bill Tom, bigger than the one they had when she wanted to go back and finish high school, longer than the one when she wanted to sing again with the gospel quartet. Only this time Shug won.

As soon as Jeanette graduated from high school, she went out to live with Sonny and his girlfriend. For a while she sang for tips at a country-western bar on the edge of town. When that fell through, he helped her get on as a maid at the Hilton. She had a portfolio made and tried the modeling agencies in Los Angeles. Once she was in the running to be those hands in the Kraft mayonnaise commercials that fold the mayonnaise into the recipe in the glass bowl.

Now the way Shug tells it, about four one morning when Jeanette was on duty at the Hilton, a call came down from the penthouse suite for fresh towels and she was sent up with them. When the door opened, she nearly screamed, because instead of one of the bodyguards, it was Him. Jeanette's heart just melted. He was wearing a blue jogging suit too small for him and holding his sunglasses in one hand. He looked so sad and tired and fat, but his eyes were still sweet and vulnerable, like those of a little lost boy. She wanted to cry, but instead she told him how much she admired him and about singing "Peace in the Valley" in the Junior Miss pageant because of him. Two big guys came up behind him like they were going to lead him away, but he yelled at them and they backed off. Then he asked Jeanette to sing it for him. She threw back her shoulders and sang, slowly and simply, just the way Danny Fisher had sung the "Alma Mater" in *King Creole*. When she finished, he smiled that famous curled half smile and said, "Darlin', I want you to work for me. You'll be with me on my next tour," and he had one of the men take down her name.

Of course, before his next tour, Elvis was dead.

Jeanette went to Graceland for his funeral and then came home to stay. To be so close to being one of the Sweet Inspirations and to have fate snatch it away: she knew the end of a dream when she saw it. Within the year, she settled down with the youngest Barndollar boy and to date has put on sixty pounds.

But Shug gets more complacently beautiful as the seasons roll on. Better than having had a chance herself, she has borne a daughter who had a chance. Any mother worth her salt would prefer such, according to Shug. That fate ruined Jeanette's chance doesn't matter much. Fate is an old friend; Shug knows its face as well as her own, knows how to live with it. Fate is spinal meningitis killing a little seven-year-old boy; it's Bill Tom uprooted like a big tree blown over in a storm; it's the King dying, when, as Shug believes, if only he'd gotten to know Jeanette, he might still be alive for us all.

So when Shug stops her cart by yours, lays her slender tanned hand on your arm, and says, "Why, hello, honey. It's so good to see you. You look so good. Isn't it a beautiful day?"—even if it's raining pitchforks you believe her. And when you ask, "How's Bill

Tom today?" and she smiles and says, "Well, I believe he's doing a little better this morning," for as long as her hand is on your arm, life seems more worth living than you thought; you feel like you can make it through whatever comes your way; as long as you don't look too deeply into her beautiful eyes.

Closing Time

It is December twenty-fourth in Blue Valley. A gray snow sky hangs low over Main Street. Inside the Bon Ton Beauty Shop, a one-story, shoe-box-shaped building, the long mirror that takes up one side wall wears a scalloped edging of spray snow. At the back of the room, a silver Christmas tree twinkles next to the Coke machine. Up front, beside the cash register, sits a basket of gift samples for customers. Stick-on bows perch on the hoods of the hair dryers that run down the center of the room. Beneath the clock on the long wall opposite the mirror, a hand-lettered sign has been taped: Closing 3 P.M. on Christmas Eve.

The clock reads two twenty-one.

The beauticians, Mona, Hazel, and Dimple, wear pink foil Christmas corsages pinned to the shoulders of their pastel pants uniforms. Hazel and Dimple display on their faces the latest in holiday makeup: glitter eye shadow, liquid base in the new winter pales, wet plum lipstick. Camilla, the shampoo girl, wears a white smock over jeans and no corsage. She has tied a bow of red and green yarn strands around her ponytail. She too wears the festive makeup.

Mona wears no makeup. Her face is sallow. There are olive circles under her eyes, eyes which dart randomly without appearing to see anything. Her bouffant hairdo is matted and sticky-looking.

LaVerne Day, a customer, pushes back the hood on her dryer and goes to stand by the picture window at the front of the shop. "I wish that Mike would hurry up. I told them over at the garage that it was a-smoking to beat sixty and only seventeen thousand miles on it. They said they'd send him right over." She fishes a pack of cigarettes and a lighter out of her blazer pocket. "John's going to kill me."

59

"It's not your fault, a durned old car," says Hazel.

"I know it," says LaVerne Day, going to sit at Hazel's station, "but tell that to him."

"Men," says Hazel, with a sidelong look at Mona, who stands next to her, rolling the hair of a second customer, Pearl Thompson. Mona allows Hazel to catch her eye but otherwise does not react.

Dimple, sorting curlers by size on the other side of Mona, says to her, "Speaking of killing, did your mama know that Lorraine?"

"Mama's kin to her," says Mona.

"Kin to her or him?" inquires Dimple shrewdly.

"Well, him," allows Mona, twirling up another length of Pearl Thompson's hair. "But Mama said she always thought a lot of her. Naw, we didn't have the news on all yesterday."

Dimple says, "They called me to do her hair, since we went to school together and all. I'm going straight over to the funeral home from here. She has such pretty hair."

"Had," Mona reminds her. She stops to massage the back of her own neck.

Pearl Thompson clucks, "You never can tell. He always seemed like such a nice boy. So nice and easy about everything."

"Way he takes his cap off and sets it back on," Dimple agrees.

"Nice can fool you," Hazel says lightly in Mona's direction.

Pursing her lips, LaVerne Day shoots smoke at the mirror. "Lord, y'all are morbid! Let's talk about Christmas."

"Well," Hazel says, "I've got fourteen people coming for dinner tonight, if I can get out of here to cook it. We're going to Richard's sister's tomorrow. Mona, you and your girls still going to your mama's for Christmas dinner?"

"We're going tomorrow night. I have to work noon at the restaurant," says Mona.

"Do you mean to tell me you're still working five days here and two at the Starlite?" Pearl exclaims.

"My girls needs a Christmas," Mona says.

There is a silence.

"Don't *he* do nothing for them, Mona?" Shug Watson, the third customer, asks from the row of dryers behind them.

"No," says Mona.

"You could take him to court," says Shug Watson.

"I did," says Mona. "Let's not talk about it anymore."

Smirking, Camilla prisses over to select a bottle of nail polish from a tray. "Reckon J.T.'s going to be spending Christmas with that other one?"

Hazel whirls and stabs Camilla in the arm with the handle of a rattail comb. Camilla gasps, and tears fill her eyes.

Mona sighs. "Oh, it's all right. It's none of my concern what he does anymore."

"Anyway, *which* other one?" says Dimple. "There were about ten of them."

"Now, y'all stop. J.T. can be sweet. He really can," Mona warns.

"You stop!" Dimple snaps. "You know what happened the last time you took him back."

"That was an accident. But don't worry, I'm really through this time. I haven't seen him in five months," says Mona. Biting her lip, she turns her head away.

"Christmas is hard on a person, when certain things have happened," Pearl Thompson says gently.

The door opens and a frail old lady, Mrs. McCormick, totters in. Her shoulders are hunched with worry. She grasps the top of her purse with both hands, like a sparrow steadying itself on a branch in the wind. She goes up to Hazel and whispers, "I got my car parked on a line. I wonder if I better change it. Do you think I ought to change it? It's parked on a line."

Abruptly, as to a child, Hazel says, "Go change it."

Obediently Mrs. McCormick totters out again.

Hazel looks at the clock and rolls her eyes up to the ceiling.

Camilla sidles past Mona, giggling. "She had to go change her car."

"You ought to tell her how you park astraddle all the time, Camilla," Dimple retorts loudly. "If she knowed how you park astraddle those lines, she might not think nothing of it."

Camilla, head down, retires to a seat in the bank of hair dryers. She takes a nail file out of the pocket of her smock and starts on a thumbnail, concentrating hard.

Dimple gets Shug Watson out from under the dryer and takes her curlers out.

Mona puts Pearl Thompson under another dryer. She nods at the clock, which reads two forty-five. "I wonder what happened to Mrs. McCormick."

"I bet she took her car home to park it," says Hazel. "We can't do her now. It's too late. We couldn't hardly do her when she first come in."

A Chevrolet pickup pulls in front of the window. It is new; iridescent letters on the radiator grille read: REBEL. In place of the front license plate there is a metal Confederate flag. A man gets out. When he walks in the shop, everyone looks at Mona. Stone-faced, Mona turns her back on the man. She takes up the broom that is leaning against the wall and sweeps hair clippings into a pile.

The man swaggers back to the Coke machine and feeds change into it. His hair is slicked back in an old-fashioned ducktail, with gray at the temples. His face is tanned, and hard-looking as a saddle. He wears faded jeans, a flannel-lined denim jacket, and dirty buck Wellington boots. He walks back to the front, takes a seat facing the window, and pops open his Coke.

No one speaks. Dimple brush-styles and sprays Shug Watson's pageboy. Hazel teases and pins LaVerne Day's French roll. Mona picks up used towels. Dimple gets Pearl Thompson out from under the dryer.

"Merry Christmas, everybody," Shug Watson says, handing Dimple a bill and putting her coat on. She goes over to the basket of customer gifts and picks up the samples one after another, considering which to take. She sneaks looks at the man.

The man takes out his wallet. He counts his money, first the bills and then the change, even the pennies. He flips through the plastic windows of the wallet, removing various cards to look at the backs, as if he is trying to establish the identity of the man whose wallet it is. He takes out his driver's license and reads it.

Hazel gathers up combs and brushes and puts them in the sterilizer. She turns on the radio and dials to an instrumental version of "O Little Town of Bethlehem." Camilla, eyes on the back of the man's head, creeps around straightening stacks of magazines.

The door opens and it is Mrs. McCormick again. She is wearing one glove. Her eyes have lost color. She blinks at the clock like a baby. It reads two fifty-nine. "I've done missed my appointment, ain't I?"

Mona is putting cans of hair spray in a drawer. The man turns around and looks at Mona in the mirror. The reflection of her eyes jerk over to meet the reflection of his. A spray can falls from her hand. When it hits the floor everyone jumps except the man, who grins. Mona stoops to retrieve it. When she stands again, a red flush is spreading up her neck.

She looks straight at Mrs. McCormick. She starts to speak but has to clear her throat before she can say, "Set down. I'll do you."

Dimple and Hazel trade glances.

LaVerne Day, who has been rummaging in her purse, comes up with two Chiclets. She tosses them in her mouth and says, "I believe I'll walk over to the garage and see what's happened to Mike. It's three. Y'all'll be wanting to close."

Slowly and distinctly Dimple tells LaVerne Day, "It's awful cold out to walk. Why don't you call them from here? You can wait a few minutes longer."

Mona scratches red patches that have appeared on her throat.

LaVerne Day chews slower. "I see what you mean, honey."

"Camilla," says Hazel suddenly, "I wonder if Mrs. Doctor Moore still wants that comb-out. I believe we could work her in after all. Why don't you give her a call?"

The man throws a quick, sweeping look over his shoulder. He slouches down in his chair and takes something out of his jacket pocket. Holding it at eye level, he turns it around, examining it from every angle. It is a white pasteboard box topped with a silver bow, of the kind used by the local jewelry store.

Shug Watson and Dimple consult in whispers. They bring over the plates of homemade candy and cookies that have been sitting on top of the beauty products display case. They make a space for them on the counter in front of Mrs. McCormick.

"The pecan dreams are LaVerne's," says Shug Watson.

"Oooooh," says everybody.

"I'm going to start my diet the day after Christmas," Dimple vows.

"I always start on New Year's," says Pearl Thompson.

"I start mine on Elvis's birthday," says Shug Watson.

They gather around the chair where, with shaking hands, Mona is sectioning off Mrs. McCormick's hair.

Camilla returns from the phone. "She says she'll be right over."

"I don't know when's the last time I've seen her," says LaVerne Day brightly. "I believe I'll wait to say hi."

"O Holy Night" is playing on the radio.

"I love that song they're singing," says Camilla.

"It's that Pavarotti," says Pearl Thompson.

"Pava how much?" asks Hazel.

"Big fat opera singer. He done a special with Loretta Lynn one time," says Dimple.

"Oh, him," says Hazel.

The man has returned the box to his jacket pocket. He picks up a magazine and puts it down. He lights a cigarette. He checks the time on his wristwatch against that on the wall clock. He taps his foot.

"I guess y'all know I used to sing in a gospel quartet," says Shug Watson. "Here is how the alto goes." She sings along on "O Holy Night." LaVerne Day pulls up chairs. She and Dimple sit down. Mona keeps working; her hands are steadier. The women pass the plates of sweets among themselves. Everyone takes one of each kind. They do not offer any to the man. But they are all watching him in the mirror.

It was six-thirty of a Sunday morning when the phone rang. I thought our business was burning down until I heard Cousin Edith's voice. Then I knew somebody had died. That bunch down in Blue Valley don't call me for nothing else.

"Now, Dreama," she said right off, "just take it easy."

"I was."

"Well, I'm sorry to call so early. But it's your Aunt Sadie."

I reached for my cigarettes on the nightstand, knowing already that Aunt Sadie was dead, Aunt Sadie that I thought would go on forever, and knowing that Cousin Edith wanted me to drag the gory details out of her. The ones you love always leave without saying good-bye. It's the bastards that linger. Edith, I thought, sit on it and twirl.

She sighed and said, "All right, honey, go on and get ahold of yourself while I talk. I was with her all yesterday evening, pore old soul, and along about eight-thirty she sets up and says, 'Oh, my God, it's Edith. Where am I?' I told her she was in the nursing home and she grabbed my arm, you wouldn't believe how strong she was, and she says, 'Go to the bank and get me thirty thousand dollars. I'm buying a goddamn ambulance and I'm wheeling out of here!' That's when I knew she wasn't at herself, you see, that profanity. So I went to tell the nurse Sadie'd went mental on me again, and when I got back, she was gone." Edith blew a tune on her nose. "They said it was her heart."

It was waking up and seeing Edith there, if you ask me. If Cousin Edith takes an interest in you, you know you're not long for this world.

I said, "Sadie wasn't crazy."

ome who would wonder about a person setting their-

hen?"

"Last week. Olivia's oldest girl was with her. Of course I don't reckon she actually meant to. My opinion, it was a judgment on them fancy gowns she wore. They wasn't proper. She caught her sleeve trying to light one of them little cigars of hers, and that gown went up like a blowtorch. Singed her hair, even."

Floyd was out eating bran flakes in front of the TV when I told him. Aunt Sadie was one of the few in the family who knew Floyd. She'd even stood up with me when we got married.

He lit a cigarette and set back rubbing his belly, where the ulcer is. "Sorry now?" he said.

"Hell, no. I'm not sorry."

"Lying." He kept watching the news.

"She wasn't there when I needed her," I said.

"That was six year ago. You should've gone to see her after she went in the nursing home."

"My conscience is clear!" I hollered.

"Not if she's your mother."

"You know good and well nobody ever thought that but me and Randall, when we was kids. And that was mostly when we was mad at Mom and Dad and wished we was in another family."

"They was more to it than that," Floyd said.

"Wasn't neither, not hard evidence. Just the fact that Aunt Sadie was staying with Mom and Dad down in Fletcher County around the time I was born. Just rumors. Plus once Mom told me she didn't think she could have any more children after Norton, so I was a nice surprise. Which I doubt, considering me and her never got along. Then after Mom got religion, Sadie moved to Charleston and they never spoke again. Why, Mom wouldn't even allow us to talk about Sadie, said she was wild and unrepentant. Which I ignored, as you well know. Now that's it, Floyd. That's all she wrote."

"Even if she just might of been, you ought to go to the funeral." Mothers is everything to Floyd. His called him Baby Floyd until after we was married. He wants to be buried by her.

I said, "I haven't been home in fifteen years and I'm not starting now. I wouldn't give that crowd the treat of looking at me. It's too late to do anything for Aunt Sadie and you know we can't afford the gas." He opened his mouth but I ran right over him. "It makes no difference to me how we're related. Anyway, if Sadie'd ever said anything, you better believe Cousin Edith would have spread it around by now. Only thing that old heifer loves better than a funeral is a scandal."

In the middle of the morning Floyd went out. We only eat two meals of a Sunday, the big one about three o'clock. All the time I was cooking, I was studying how to go to Blue Valley, but I didn't see no way. Floyd came back at three ten sharp; and when I set down at the table, there was a hundred-dollar bill under my coffee cup.

"Why, look-a-there," he said, and rolled them old bedroom eyes.

"Where'd you get it?"

"Never mind. It's for you to go to Blue Valley. I filled up the car too. Day after tomorrow, you're going."

Let's face it, the man's got a heart as big as a baseball park. And you can't fool him.

It's four hours by car to Blue Valley. I hate the place. There was nothing to do there as a kid, except things they never forgot you did. Sadie always told me I deserved better; and when I decided to run away at sixteen, she sent me the bus fare.

When I got to the church, the parking lot was full. Norton and my cousin Harold was lurking in the vestibule. Norton had that walleyed look he gets around sick or dead people. His hands hung at his sides like hams. "Hello, Sister," was all he said. We're black sheep and white sheep to each other.

Never at a loss for words, Harold said, "Well, Dreama, I swan. Well, I'll say," and he give me a hug.

Then Cousin Hazel and Cousin Edith come creeping up. Those two have been hit with the same club. Cousin Hazel's mouth was going open and shut like a goldfish's, on account of my mink stole and lizard pumps, which they don't have to know I got off a guy that owed us money.

"Lord, Dreama, we didn't expect you. And you look wonderful."

Edith took my arm and said, "So does Sadie. Let's go in and see her." Edith kind of grows on you. Like a fungus.

They had Sadie surrounded by big carnation-and-gladioli arrangements in spite of the fact that for forty years she'd said she didn't want no flowers at her funeral. Right in front was a bunch of wildflowers that looked like a kid had arranged them. That one made sense, if anybody only knew it. Sadie was the wildest flower ever to grow in Blue Valley. Besides, she loved daylilies. Long years ago, there was lots of them around Grandpa and Grandma's house on the road to Breathitt's Mill, where Sadie and Mom and Bithie and Garland and Clinton, not to mention poor Aunt Iris that died so young, was born.

"Didn't they do a good job on her?" Hazel says.

It was the only time I felt like crying. Aunt Sadie was a fixy woman, as vain as you please. And here they had her in a mustard-shit green dress, with her mouth painted up like a polecat's butt that's been eating pokeberries. She looked like a comic valentine.

"Her favorite color was pink," I said.

"Pink is a lovely color," says Hazel.

The whole town was there. People didn't exactly like Sadie but they come to respect her, which is about as lucky as you can get in a dipstick burg like Blue Valley. Respect: now there's a rathole to throw everything down.

The front row, where immediate family sits, was empty, of course. Sadie's son Carson, that she always called the Lout, is stationed in Alaska. I sat about midway back. That oldest girl of Harold's, Risa, was playing the organ. I sort of sang along in my head, through a couple of verses of "Rock of Ages" and "When the Roll Is Called Up Yonder." Then all of a sudden, I noticed the organ was playing,

> Well you came home drunk last night
> You smelled like Gypsy Rose
> Well I don't know just
> Where you been
> But Slim brought home your clothes—

It was slow and churchy, with the cello stop out, but it was definitely one of the songs Sadie used to sing in the roadhouses out West. I give the congregation the hairy eyeball, but nobody seemed to be noticing the music. They sure never heard Sadie sing it. That part of her life ended a couple of years ago after that last husband died and she got so broke down and had to come back to Blue Valley to live. By now the kid was on "Amazing Grace" and tapering off, as one of those new-fangledy preachers with blow-dried hair stepped up to the microphone.

He talked about some other woman named Sadie, not the one I knew. The nice old lady he was slightly acquainted with would have called or wrote during them two years I had to quit work to take care of Mom, at the same time Floyd was laid off work for nine months, snoring on the davenette or out boozing. His Sadie would've been there one of those days when I would have give an arm and a leg to get out of that house for a couple of hours, and not have to keep locking doors so Mom wouldn't wander off in her nightgown, or rush around looking for the scissors when she hid them, or keep her from smashing tomatoes against the windows. Aunt Bithie telephoned once in a while; and even Norton had the sense to send money and to visit once, though he never spoke to Mom the whole weekend. Then a year and a half after Mom died, which Sadie didn't even come to the funeral or send flowers, she pops in with a two-pound box of candy and a policeman husband from Arizona, as if none of it ever happened. Looking at her laying there so peaceful, I thought, I'm one up on you now, Sadie. You're going to owe me one for eternity. Thankfully the service ended then; and we filed out to "Toot, Toot, Tootsie," played on the brass stops.

I laid for that Risa just outside the door, while the rest of the relatives was maneuvering to see who got to ride with the mortician. Directly she come out smiling to herself, a skinny little old thing of about seventeen, with limp red hair down to her shoulders and crooked-cut bangs. Her polyester suit was too short, and her spindly legs made her shoes look as big as Daisy Duck's. Somebody needed to do her over.

"I'm your Cousin Dreama," I said. "Where'd you learn to play the organ like that?"

"I know who you are. Mrs. Cotter taught me to chord. I sorta picked the rest up." Her eyes was on my stole.

Risa's mother, that rat's ass Olivia, hollered for her to come on.

"How'd you like to ride with me?" I said.

You'd have thought she won the lottery. Said, "That's an Imperial, ain't it? Man, I'd love to."

Once the procession started I said, "Hey, you throwed some different songs in there."

She kind of shrunk together, like some animal camouflaging itself.

"It's okay, I'm glad you did."

She licked her lips. "I just thought she ought to have some of her own music."

"Did you know her real well?" I asked.

"I took her on as a project. We had to make friends with a senior citizen for social studies. I visited with her and run errands."

"Sadie wouldn't have liked being a project."

"We got to be friends. I kept going to see her after it was over."

"Edith said you was there when she burned herself."

She run her hands over the upholstery on either side of her. "It was just a little accident. I threw water on it."

"She talk to you a lot?"

"I guess so."

"Did she ever talk about me?" I asked.

She chewed a hangnail, making up her mind about something. "She talked about the old days. Told me a lot of stuff."

My nerves started twanging. "Did she talk to the nurses too? Old folks can get kind of mouthy."

"No'm, she just talked to me as far as I know." At the next stoplight she looked at me. She didn't ever seem to blink, like a snake. "Did Great-aunt Sadie ever tell you about me, Cousin Dreama?"

"No."

She faced forward. The air went out of her. At the cemetery she got out of the car and then leaned back in with this funny little smile. "Aunt Sadie liked your letters. She kept all of them."

"What do you mean 'all'?"

"Ever one you ever wrote, I guess. She had them in a big box in her room. Thanks for the ride."

I clawed that bottle out of my purse and swallowed one drop for each kidney. I couldn't begin to remember everything that was in those letters. Not the recent ones, which was just polite. But all the ones before eight years ago, when Sadie abandoned me in my time of trouble. Except for Floyd, Sadie is the only person I ever confided in. I never dreamed she'd keep them. She never even saved last year's shoes.

I wasn't planning to go to Wilma Dean's after the cemetery, but I lost the kid in the crowd. I didn't find her at Wilma Dean's either, but over by the buffet table I ran into Alma Frodge, that works at the nursing home. Alma wears her hair up in a little cowpat and her front teeth hang out like laundry on a line. She told me Sadie'd signed everything over to the nursing home, so there wasn't no need for a will. The only things left was her gowns and one box of personal effects, which was upstairs in Wilma Dean's closet.

"I'd love to have something to remember her by," I said. "Why, she might even have kept a letter or two of Bithie's."

"There wasn't nothing like that, Dreama. Only stuff like a manicure set and powder and earrings and her Bible. Aren't you going to eat nothing? That banana-split cake is delicious."

"No, thanks, Alma, you never know who's washed their socks in the cake bowl," I said, and I dropped her like a dirty shirt.

Inside of two minutes I was in Wilma Dean's bedroom with the door locked, thumbing through that Bible. I'd forgot about it, though when I moved Mom and Dad off the farm, I noticed it was missing. It was the little one from Mom and Sadie's side of the family. When I found the family record pages, the marriage page was there and the death page. But the page of births was tore out.

When I'm upset, I drive. So I wandered around saying my goodbyes and then I hit the road. At first I just meant to drive around town and then swing back and get ahold of that little Risa again. But before I knew it, I was headed home. Floyd's not the brightest little person walking around, but he knows how to listen; and I needed to talk. About ten miles out of town I turned on the radio and started singing at the top of my lungs. Then it hit me Sadie was gone and I commenced to cry. Another fifty miles and I'd figured out that one of the reasons I never asked her in recent years about her being my mother was I didn't think she'd die with unfinished business. So not knowing was a kind of guarantee that I still had time to find out. I should have remembered that Aunt Sadie was as independent as a hog on ice.

I'd talk to her for a while and then I'd cry some more. "You left it up to Mom to tell me, didn't you?" I said. "Well, I asked Mom. Because kids hear things. Things is said behind your back. And every time she'd answer out of the Bible. 'A wicked doer giveth heed to false lips; and a liar giveth ear to a naughty tongue,' she'd say. Or, 'I have nourished and brought up children, and they have rebelled against me.' And once when I kept on at her, she called me 'thou child of the devil.' But you, Sadie, I wasn't supposed to ask you. You was supposed to tell me." After a while I could hardly think how to drive, I was so upset. Not counting Floyd, I was alone in the world now: too old to be an orphan and too young for Social Security. "And that little red-headed varmint of Olivia's knows something," I said. "You betrayed me to her. My trouble was and always will be, I loved you too much. I should've learned to be as hard-hearted as you." After two hours of such carrying on, I needed a break, so I stopped at this little off-brand restaurant and ordered scrambled eggs, sliced tomatoes, and coffee. I had my compact out and was fixing my face when Risa walked in, pulled out the chair opposite me, and set down.

"It was too hot to stay in the car. I was on the floor in the back," she said in this little reedy voice.

"Well, I'll take vanilla," I said. We stared at each other, it sinking in on me what she'd overheard. But the kid had her own problems. Her bottom lip was stuck out far enough for a jaybird to build a nest on it. By and by it commenced to tremble; and two big old tears rolled down her cheeks.

"What is it?" I said.

She shrugged and looked down at her lap.

"Your mama is probably already looking for you."

"They don't care about me. They never have." Her freckles was as big as pennies against that white skin. She started to sob, real open-faced, with her eyes wide. "Please take me with you. Please. You've always been my idol. I remember once you come to Christmas dinner wearing a red wool suit with a fur collar and a hat with a veil. You looked like a movie star and we drove you to the train station afterwards. Ever since then, I've wanted to be like you, I swear to God. Don't take me back. I'll do anything." She went to boohooing in her hands.

"Suppose I do. Just suppose."

She stopped crying like that and hitched her chair up. "Why, I could stay with you until I get on my feet. I can type sixty words a minute and take shorthand. It won't take long. See, I belong in a big city, like you do. And I'm aiming to travel like you and Aunt Sadie done, too. She told me all about her living out West and about you and Cousin Floyd traveling with the carnival."

The waitress brought my coffee and another menu.

"Look here," I said to the kid, "you want to cry, you just trot over to that big wailing wall they got in China. Don't waste your tears on me. You don't remember any such thing as me coming home for Christmas. You was only seventeen months old."

She slapped her purse on the table and her face changed like in those werewolf movies. "I got those letters. I know everything about you, Cousin Dreama. And I don't care who I tell."

"Purse isn't big enough to hold all of them."

"I got the important ones."

I blowed on my coffee and swallowed a slug. When I lit my cigarette, I let my hands shake. "You got the Bible too? It's got stuff wrote in it I wouldn't want to get out."

"I got it."

I come across that table like a tornado and had that purse before she knowed what happened. "You little shit, I'm a good mind to snatch you baldheaded," I said. "That Bible is in Wilma Dean's closet."

"Give me that back!" She was scared now.

The waitress fluttered up. "Is everything all right?"

"Honey," I said to her, "do you like hot coffee?"

"Why, yes," the waitress answered.

"So do I and this ain't. Go get me another cup." With that, I dumped the purse out. The usual trash, but no letters and no birth page. But there was a daylily from the wildflower bouquet at the funeral. I picked it up.

"Give me that!" Risa hollered with pure hate.

"You thought a lot of Aunt Sadie, didn't you?" I said. "Really. I'm talking to you straight now."

She sagged all over. After a long time she said, "Sadie said sometimes people get born into the wrong family. We used to pretend like she was my grandmother and you was my mother. Only you let her down. You never called nor wrote that whole last year."

Which just shows you what kind of viper she is, bringing that up. But kind of gently I said, "How about them letters?"

"That's how Aunt Sadie set herself on fire. She got to thinking about dying and went to burn a bunch of stuff in the wastebasket. Other things besides letters too. Miss Frodge wouldn't let her have dinner that night for being a nuisance. But she got it all burned."

"Did you see any of it?"

"Old junk, it looked like to me. I don't think she hardly knew what she was doing. She tore a page out of that Bible you was talking about, and burned it."

"Did you see it?" I asked.

"Yes. It was blank."

I looked out the window. Even if Floyd stopped at the Eagles for a drink, he'd be home by now. There was a gum tree by the edge of the parking lot that had already lost its leaves. It cast a long shadow that was different from itself. Some of the branches that was separated on the tree crossed each other in the shadow. Family trees and shadow family trees, I thought, and who knows which is which? The kid would hurt me sooner or later, and I would probably hurt her. But hurt is better than nothing; and there was a chance it might turn out better than that. While Risa ordered herself a hamburger, I called Blue Valley and told them I'd send her home when her and I got good and ready. Then I called Floyd and told him what Aunt Sadie had willed us.

Stealing Sugar

The first week they were in the new house, Emily got a puppy. They were lucky to get the house. Men back from the war were settling down, starting families, and going to Blue Valley College on the GI Bill. If it hadn't been for Emily's father singing tenor in the Methodist choir next to a man from the bank, they never would have had a chance at the Warren house before it went on the market. Though as small as the doodlebug house on the west side, where they had lived since Emily was a baby, the Warren house was in the neighborhood directly south of the college, where so many faculty and the better sort of townspeople lived. At last, said Emily's mother, they would be able to Live Graciously.

One night before bedtime Emily was playing dolls in the musty hall, with the front door open to a steady summer rain. When she heard the whimpering she ran straight outside in her nightgown, the rain laying cold pennies on her back. A pinkish tan puppy crouched against the base of the house, blinking in the rain-spangled porch light.

Squatting in the mud, Emily trapped it against her chest. The puppy was slippery and sprawling and smelled like earthworms. Its head lolled over her arm as she carried it into the living room to show her parents.

"I love you, little puppy," she whispered in its ear. To her parents she said, "Look at my surprise!"

Emily's mother jumped out of her chair. Her sewing basket spilled from her lap, buttons wheeling in all directions.

"Oh, no! Where in the world? Norton, get it away from her!"

Emily's father, who had been reading the newspaper, spread the want-ad section across his lap and took the dog onto it. When he got a good look through the bottom of his bifocals, his face seemed to climb backwards over itself.

"It was by the porch. Can I get it some hamburger?" Emily asked.

"Lord God, it's got the mange," said her mother to her father. "I can't imagine a dog like that belonging to anyone around *here.* "

Her father poked at the puppy's belly, which seemed too big and round for the rest of it. He clenched and unclenched his teeth and said to Emily's mother, "No. Where's the flashlight? You'll have to hold it."

"I will?"

"Yes, you will."

Emily's mother turned on her. "Get upstairs this very instant and take off that filthy gown. And get in the tub. I'll be up in a minute."

"But I already—"

"Move," said Emily's father, and Emily moved.

But she did not get in the tub. Standing at the window of her room she looked down on the backyard, where soon a flashlight beam moved from the house to the woodpile. Her father walked in front, bareheaded in the rain, holding the puppy by the scruff of its neck. The puppy curled its body away from him the way a slug would curl away from a sharp twig. When her father dropped it on the ground, the puppy let out a breathless yelp like her crybaby doll. Her mother followed with an umbrella. Face averted so that her husband kept having to shout at her to mind her business, she held the light on the puppy while he clubbed it three times with a piece of kindling. Each time the club fell, Emily's stomach jerked all by itself.

Later, when Emily had been bathed again and tucked in bed by her mother, who did not speak to her except to say good night, her father came and sat on the edge of her bed.

Pushing back her hair he said in his gentle voice, "Baby, the puppy was very sick. The poor thing couldn't have lived, so Daddy had to put it to sleep. You wouldn't want it to suffer, would you?"

Halfway through her bath, Emily had understood what she had seen. She rolled her face away from her pillow. "But why?"

"It's the law of the jungle, honey. Only the strong survive. When Daddy lived on the farm, sometimes there would get to be too many barn cats. They ate up all the mousie-wousies in the corn crib and we couldn't feed them. So, your Grandpa would tell Daddy or Uncle Randall to shoot some. Otherwise they would starve. 'Shoot them while they're sleeping in the sun,' he'd say. That was the most merciful."

"And you only shot the weak ones?"

"Well . . . of course."

Tears spilling, Emily sat up into his arms.

He folded her tight in his bear hug. "These things happen. That's the way life is."

"But he was *mine*," Emily wailed into his chest.

Her father's voice turned playful. "Here, let's see something. Do you know how to tell if somebody steals sugar?" Through the sheet, he grabbed her thigh just above the knee in a pincer grasp. "If you steal sugar, you'll flinch." His thumb and forefinger suddenly dug hard between her muscles.

Emily's leg jumped. "Ow!"

Her father laughed. "Uh oh, I guess you steal sugar. Let's see, are you sure?" And he squeezed again.

The pinch made Emily's leg hurt in a prickly way and she cried harder. But in a little while she was laughing through her tears, and her father was pleased and went away.

The next week she and her mother found the little park. Soft with beds of petunias, marigolds, and ageratum, it lay on the sloping greenway between Crescent Boulevard, along which the Georgian buildings of the college were ranged, and College Street, where the Farnsworth mansion stood behind its iron picket fence. Except for a workman pruning the cotoneaster hedge, no one was about. Emily's mother sat on a park bench and turned her face up to the sun while Emily ran from swings to slide to merry-go-round.

Presently the front door of the Farnsworth mansion opened and a girl came out, a golden spaniel shuffling at her heels. For the first time in her life, Emily was aware of a child as beautiful. A white ribbon held the girl's long, reddish brown hair back from a face as still and open as a deer's. Tall for her age, she moved with a lilting, fluid walk toward the workman. Emily, who had never cared about clothes, suddenly saw that clothes too could be lovely, in this case a short-sleeved cream sweater over a pleated plaid skirt, knee socks, and highly burnished penny loafers such as the high school girls wore around the soda fountain at Baird Drug. On the girl from the mansion, the shoes looked pretty enough to be magical. Around her neck she wore a single pearl on a thin gold chain.

At the end of the hedge, the girl stooped to grasp the collar of the dog and whisper something in its ear. For a moment, with her eyes on the workman, her face sharpened like a bird's. Then she straightened and said in a clear, carrying voice, "Parnell, Dad-Dad says you're to help Bertha with those boxes now." Folding her arms, she watched until the workman had wordlessly gathered up his tools and started across the street. Then she turned her attention to Emily, who sat motionless in a swing.

"Want a push?"

Her name was Adele and she was seven. After they played on the swings Adele suggested the teeter-totter.

"It's called a seesaw," Emily said gravely.

"I have different words for things because I'm not the salt of the earth like Bertha is. I was born in Paris, France. Can you speak French?" said Adele.

Emily could not.

"*Je suis tres contente de faire votre connaissance,*" said Adele. "*Il y a beaucoup de sots dans le monde.*"

Later as they were sitting on the bench with Emily's mother, who had given them each a stick of Juicy Fruit, the front door of the mansion opened again and out came a tall, balding man with a fringe of white hair and ruddy cheeks. Unlike any man Emily had ever seen, he wore yellow slacks and a green pullover, colors for girls.

Striding up to Emily's mother, he extended a firm hand. "I see you've met my granddaughter. I'm David Farnsworth."

"Dad-Dad, this is Emily. May she come to play?" said Adele.

David Farnsworth beamed down at Emily. The way the sunlight danced on his gold-rimmed glasses and along the crowns on his teeth made her think of Santa Claus. "Well, now, I don't know. Let's see, Emily. Are you a Republican or a Democrat?"

Emily plumped her fists on her hips. "I'm a 'publican! President Truman is rotten as a peanut and stubborn as a Missouri mule!"

"Emily," murmured her mother.

"Ah ha! And who taught you that?"

"My Grandpa Forrester."

"He sounds like a good man," said David Farnsworth, and he gave Emily a dime for ice cream.

That night at dinner Emily's mother said, "David Farnsworth *himself.* I nearly died, you can imagine: wearing this old dress and my hair not washed. But didn't I tell you we would meet people here? Emily is invited over to play tomorrow. She told him we were Republicans and he gave her a dime!"

Emily's father winked at her. "That's my girl."

"I feel sorry for little Adele, though. You know her mother committed suicide and then the grandparents had an awful time getting custody. The father was some French artist and wanted to raise Adele in France. Of course they couldn't put up with that."

"What's suicide?" asked Emily.

Spooning gravy over his pork chops her father said, "When you commit suicide, you kill yourself."

"Why?"

"Because you don't want to take responsibility for your life. It takes a pretty weak sister to do something like that."

"How do you kill yourself?"

Emily's mother tapped her on the wrist. "Eat your lima beans, if you want any cherry cobbler."

"I will. But how—?"

"*And,* we will talk about pleasant things at the dinner table."

"So Martha," said Emily's father with a chuckle, "you've seen the light, have you? A Republican at last."

Adele's grandmother was called Mimi. Her pinkish blond hair marched to the nape of her neck in strict waves, and her limp, gauzy dresses made Emily think of wilted flowers. At the kitchen table she gave them ginger ale in heavy glasses and saucers of oyster crackers and nodded and smiled when they minded their manners. Otherwise she busied herself visiting with other old ladies in the parlor or talking on the telephone or lying down in her room with wet bags of chamomile tea on her eyelids. All of these activities required Emily and Adele to be neither seen nor heard. One day, while they were slipping past the parlor door being Indians, they overheard a woman say to Mimi, "When I see how much trouble children are, I wonder why there are so many of them in the world."

"I'm sure I can't tell you," returned Mimi. "They're nothing but heartbreak."

That day Adele showed Emily a trunk in the attic containing long shiny gowns with net petticoats, evening sweaters edged in pearls, bathing suits with hard strips sewn in the bosoms to make them pooch out, a long, black velvet evening coat.

"These clothes belong to the Queen of Heartbreak but she doesn't mind if we play princess with them. She sings me to sleep every night and then we go places in my dreams. We go east of the sun and west of the moon," said Adele, and touched the pearl at her throat. "She gave me this and I never take it off."

Every morning Adele had a new game ready when Emily arrived, with the roles already decided. When they played in the antique car in the garage, Adele was the chauffeur and Emily was an orphan being taken to live with relatives she had never seen. When Bertha fixed them café au lait and jam bread, Adele was the rich hostess and Emily the visitor come to call. Once Dad-Dad let them dance ballet in the library to one of his classical records while he shoved aside his work and pretended to be the audience. Adele was a beautiful dying swan and Emily a comical duck paddling around the edge of the lake. If Parnell was not working in the garden, they hunted butterflies. Whenever Parnell was around, Adele would not go outside and particularly would not let Duchess, the spaniel, go out.

In a patch of unmowed grass at the bottom of the garden stood a playhouse that had belonged to Adele's mother and her mother's sister, whom no one had seen in years. A tree limb that had smashed the roof line long ago still lay across it, growing lichens crinkly as witches' skin, and both windows were jaggedly broken. Mildew stained the walls inside and out. Checked gingham curtains hung in pale shreds and rabbit droppings littered the grimy floor. Emily had the idea to clean up the playhouse and make it the Best Friends Clubhouse. They began work on a Tuesday, but on Wednesday

Adele could not play. When Emily arrived at the playhouse on Thursday morning with her toy broom, Adele's mood had changed. "It's dumb to clean it up. There's too much work and I'll get dirty," she said in a thin whine, picking at the dotted-swiss material of her dress.

"Don't you have any play clothes? Why do you always wear dresses?"

"Why can't we play at your house?"

"It's funner here," Emily said, quickly plying her broom.

"We never go to your house," Adele fretted. "You could invite me every Wednesday."

Emily swept harder. By now she could hardly bear to be separated from Adele overnight, but some days Adele could not ask her in. They could never play on Wednesdays, when Mimi and Bertha went to town to do the week's shopping and Adele said Mimi said Dad-Dad didn't want to ride herd on them.

In fact Emily had already asked her mother about Wednesdays.

"Not until I get new living room curtains and a slipcover for Daddy's armchair, at the very least. And to tell you the truth, the kitchen ought to be painted too. Adele is used to a much nicer house."

"But we wouldn't care. We'd play outside."

"Oh, *outside*. Where your father has that wood stacked up like he was still living on the farm. It looks just plain tacky, don't tell him I said so."

Now Emily said, "Mama doesn't want you to come until our house is fixed up. But you wouldn't care, would you? Your bed smells like pee pee."

Something hit her on the back and bounced to the floor. A walnut. Behind her a high, tight voice said, "It does not. *Salaud.* Take it back."

Emily turned. Adele's eyes were wild, as if a house were burning behind them.

Emily felt about to cry. "Please don't be ignorant with me, Adele."

"*Tu est sot.* Go home. I don't like you anymore." Dropping to the filthy floor, Adele scooted on her bottom backwards into a corner and stuck her thumb in her mouth. Her eyelids drooped and she scratched herself hard in a place Emily wasn't allowed to touch on her own body.

"I take it back, I take it back!" said Emily.

Adele's hand stopped. She opened her eyes and looked off, out the broken window.

Emily squatted in front of her. "Want to know if you steal sugar?" Without warning she grabbed Adele's dust-streaked leg the way her father had done to her. "See? Your leg jumped. That means you steal sugar. See?" Emily laughed big like a clown and jumped Adele's leg again.

Adele took her thumb out of her mouth. "I don't steal sugar. I don't steal anything," she said coldly.

"No, it means you steal sugar," Emily repeated, wondering why the game wasn't working.

Adele sat up. "It means you'll get blamed whether you did or not. Nobody will believe you didn't." Drawing both legs up under her skirt, she turned her shoulders into the corner and rested her forehead in the angle. Finally Emily gave up and went home.

For days there was no color in the world. Emily ate and slept and played the same as before she had met Adele, but when she looked out the window, nothing had a name anymore. Her mother, who had decided she didn't like a single stick of furniture they owned, was too busy moving things around and studying the Montgomery Ward catalog to remark on how quiet Emily was. One morning, she called Emily to the front door.

"Look, someone's left you a basket, and I'll bet I know who. It's like a May basket except that this isn't May Day. Here, I found it right on the doormat."

Under the dining table Emily took the basket apart. Adele had painted Emily's name on the side, surrounding it with a crescent moon, stars, cats, and butterflies with faces. Every kind of blossom from the Farnsworth garden was crammed into the basket. Emily took them out one by one, smelled them, and stroked the dying petals. At the bottom of the basket she found a folded piece of paper with a heart drawn on it. Inside lay Adele's pearl necklace.

Emily slipped the necklace over her head. In the kitchen her mother was talking on the telephone and did not hear her leave the house.

She rang a long time at the Farnsworths' back door before she noticed that Mimi's car was gone and that Bertha's work light over the kitchen sink was out. Then she remembered it was Wednesday, when they went together to town.

On the second floor, Adele's windows were open. "Adele? Adele!" Emily called, and thought she heard an answering noise. She waited. Maybe Adele was fooling. She imagined Adele hiding behind her bedroom door, poised to spring out laughing when Emily walked in.

Edging the back door open, Emily slid into the long, cool hallway. Like an Indian she stole along the thick carpet and around the big newel post at the foot of the stairs leading to the second floor. There another sound made her hesitate—voices from Adele's room.

Like water seeping into her shoes when she stood in a puddle, a sad feeling moved from the dark hall through her skin and she remembered another dim time when she had listened and looked without being seen. Once during the night when she had gotten up to go to the bathroom, through the door to her parents' bedroom she had seen her father draping a washcloth over the little lamp on the nightstand. The room took on a spooky glow in which she could barely see her mother lying in bed, shoulders strangely bare above the bed covers. Then her father, wearing only his pajama bottoms, had pulled the door shut without seeing Emily. What she remembered most was that although they had still looked like her parents, in that moment they had somehow been two other people.

Emily tiptoed up the stairs until she was on the landing outside Adele's door.

"—have to do what I say," said a voice that sounded mostly like Dad-Dad's, but low and fuzzy. "Your mother liked to do it. She was good, she was excellent, but you must do it better or I'll have Parnell put a rope around Duchess's neck. He'll hang her in the garage until her eyes bulge out. Come on, baby. Be my little geisha."

Emily stepped to the doorway.

Dressed only in a bathrobe, Dad-Dad was sitting on Adele's bed. Adele was sitting astraddle his lap. Her face was powdered dead white. Her eyes were ringed with mascara and her cheeks and lips were painted red. She was naked and Dad-Dad was pushing her hands down into his lap.

Adele raised her head and looked straight at Emily. But it was not Adele inside the sad clown face. No one was in there.

Dad-Dad's head turned. With a cry he threw Adele off him. Emily ran down the stairs, her feet barely skimming the carpet, along the hall, and out the back door. Behind her, the door crashed against the wall, and something made of glass shattered. She flew down the street, shot inside the house and up the stairs to her room. Flinging herself down on the floor, she pressed her hot face hard against the cool wood. Her heart pounded like horses' hooves. For a long time she sensed nothing else. Then, little by little, sound returned. The curtain cord bobbed against the sill. Birds twittered in the tree outside her window. In a little while her mother called her to lunch.

At the kitchen table, her mother was leafing through a house and garden magazine while she ate. Emily took her sandwich and milk back to her room and sat it on the dresser. She got out her box of plastic horses and spread them on the floor, then made little hills and tunnels in her throw rug. Beauty was her favorite horse. All afternoon Beauty led the herd away from the men who wanted to round them up. The men were clever and never showed themselves, but they were everywhere. Over and over Beauty led the colts into a cave. Then the big horses led the men away from the cave. Downstairs in the kitchen the radio came on for the afternoon serials and the aroma of baking cookies ascended through the floor register. The smell made Emily hungry and she was eating her sandwich at last when the front doorbell rang.

"Mr. Farnsworth! Please come in!"

Jumping in bed, Emily pulled the covers over her head. Voices buzzed for a long time. When at last the front door opened and shut again, she tensed for the sound of her mother's footsteps.

In the kitchen, the radio snapped off. The house came to a halt. Outside, the sunlight took on a grayish cast. When Emily had done something bad and they were waiting for her father to come home and be told, this was the way the house felt. She was going to get a spanking. Just thinking about it made her backside scrunch up like sizzling bacon. Her father's hand was bigger than her bottom. When it landed, the explosion of pain would knock her out of her body at first, so that she would only be able to open and shut her mouth soundlessly, like a goldfish fallen onto the rug. As soon as her breath returned and she could cry, her father would shout, "Crying are you? Then I'll give you some more to cry about. Damn crying women! All my life I've been plagued by them!" so that she would have to choke back the tears, intensifying the pain radiating through her body. The unshed tears would make her insides feel swollen and bruised.

She slept, woke, and slept again. Then her father's voice called her full name up the stairs.

Her mother stood in the middle of the living room with her arms crossed tightly over her bib apron. Her father sat in his armchair, head bowed, hands hanging between his knees. When Emily came into the room he slowly raised his head, gave her a long look, and lowered it again.

Her mother said to her, "Mr. Farnsworth has been to see me. I was very disappointed to hear what he had to say." To Emily's father she said, "In the first place, she went up there without my permission. In the second, she knocked a vase off a table and ran away without admitting she broke it. It's blue satin glass and has been in Mrs. Farnsworth's family for generations."

Her father grimaced at the floor.

"And furthermore," her mother's voice was trembling now, "he found them playing nasty games that were Emily's idea. He was kind enough to spare me the details, but I got a good enough picture. Where could she have learned such a thing?"

Emily's father waved a hand. "Kids. . . ."

"Was it that McBrayer boy down the street?" Emily's mother demanded of her.

Emily could not think of any words.

Her mother said louder, "And that's not all. No sirree. To top it all off, she stole a necklace that belonged to Adele's poor mother!"

Emily's hand flew to her neck. "I didn't. Adele gave it to me."

"For heaven's sake, Emily! It was the only thing Adele had of her mother's. They had to sell all the other jewelry in Paris just to live. She wouldn't give that away." Emily's mother raised her apron to her face and began to cry into it.

Her father's jaw muscles worked. Still looking at the floor he asked in a flat voice, "What kind of games were they?"

"They were exposing themselves! I just don't understand it! I'm so ashamed!" cried her mother.

"But it wasn't me. It was Dad-Dad and Adele," Emily said.

Slowly, as if he had aged during the conversation, her father got to his feet. "So," he said, "you're a liar too." Now she would get the spanking, Emily thought, her back stiffening.

Instead, her father left the house. Emily's mother went to the window and pulled the curtain aside. "Oh, dear God," she said.

When Emily's father returned, he was carrying a limb he had broken off the apple tree.

Emily's breath whistled cold in her nostrils.

Her mother said quickly, "He wouldn't accept payment for the vase. We just have to return the necklace and keep Emily from ever going up there again. Anyway, he's decided to send Adele away. Tomorrow, in fact. He's found a camp that will take her late, and after that she's going to boarding school. He said the children in this town are all little hoodlums. Please, Norton, I'll see that Emily—"

"Shut up," he said absently, as if Emily's mother were some passerby who had made a comment.

Emily spread her fingers over her buttocks.

Her father looked down at her and sighed hugely. Laying the branch across the coffee table, he took off his suit coat, folded it carefully, and draped it over the back of the armchair. To Emily there was something funny about his face. It looked almost like one of his storytelling faces, when he was *making* himself be serious. But that couldn't be right. He couldn't be playing. Now he removed his tie and dress shirt and placed them carefully atop the coat. Standing in his undershirt and trousers, he gave Emily a look of such sad, melting sweetness, that she thought her heart would stop.

"Honey, your poor old daddy has a confession to make. I'm stupid. Mama just isn't capable of teaching you to be a good girl and Daddy should have seen that. Of course Daddy has tried his best to teach you too. I've read stories to you and taken you for walks and taught you to play mumblety-peg. But I guess I've spent too much time trying to make sure we have enough to eat and can afford this nice house. If you've misbehaved and lied, it's because

I'm a bad Daddy. You're my responsibility." Handing Emily the limb, he knelt before her and bowed his head. Through his dark hair she could see that the skin of his crown was as pink as a baby's. "Hit me until your arm is tired, until you draw blood. That's what I deserve."

On the mantel, the little white clock ticked slower and slower.

"No," Emily quavered.

Emily's mother giggled. Grabbing the branch away from Emily, she tapped her husband playfully on each shoulder. "Bad boy. Bad, bad boy. He's just teasing, aren't you, Norton? Daddy's joking, Emily. You aren't supposed to hit Daddy."

Joking, thought Emily. How could he be joking? After Dad-Dad did that to Adele and made it seem like Emily's fault. After nobody believed her and Adele had to go away. After the puppy had to be killed. Yes, the puppy too. Her mother had stood right there with the flashlight and let the puppy die. Daddies were always right. So her mother was the bad, stupid one.

She flung herself at her mother, biting, kicking, scratching, hitting. "I hate you! I hate you!" she screamed as, behind her, she heard her father laughing under his breath.

"That's my little spitfire. That's my girl," he said, and when she heard the warmth surge back into his voice, Emily hit even harder, so that nothing and nobody would ever come between her and her father again.

Blanche Long Explains How Lucky Honey Taylor Is

Back when, the word you heard applied to Honey Taylor the most was *lucky*. Maybe people should have called her Lucky instead of Honey. Of course I've known her so long that I sometimes think of her as Ruth, which is her real name. Not often, but sometimes.

I won't tell you how long ago it was, but the college hired both of us the same year, me in the library and Honey to teach freshman home economics. Honey is from a farm over around Clayton Springs. When she was young she had nice skin and fine brown hair in soft curls, but that was it for looks. She was typical of the plain, bright women of my day who didn't have a boyfriend to take up their study time and so kept on studying until, almost accidentally, they became teachers.

Honey and I each had a room at Mrs. Wolfford's. It wasn't a place you'd want to live in forever; there was a man who left hairs in the bathtub. So after a few months I got married and Honey (or Ruth, as she was called then) took Mrs. Vestal's upstairs apartment.

Mrs. Wolfford and Mrs. Vestal, both of whom took in roomers, were widows. There was also a Mrs. Johnson living across the street from the college who served dinner and supper to the single teachers. She had an invalid husband. All these women, and others like them, mothered the single men and women in town. The family was the dominant pattern in people's minds then. If you were a married woman without a family of your own, you were likely to think of offering food or shelter to others, who became your family. If you were a single woman, you sought out the kind of family they provided. It was during the war. We all gave Mrs. Johnson our ration coupons and we ate very well. Good old farm cooking; you can't get brown speckled eggs like that anymore.

Pascal Dupre ate there too. He taught at the college lab school and some people thought that he was the smartest man in town, but mostly it was his background that made them assume that. What you have to understand is that Blue Valley is in the hills. It's not really southern, so much as it's mountain. Mountain culture doesn't care if Sherman burned Atlanta. We don't wring our hands over not being able to get good help. Help is for the old, the infirm, and the Farnsworths, who own nearly everything in town but our cemetery plots and don't know what else to do with their money. This is a town where even Mrs. Doctor Tate cans her own beans and is proud of it. Lots of people still fade their jeans the old-fashioned way, instead of buying jeans that are already faded. Nevertheless we give aristocrats their due. As another teacher friend of mine says, our ancestors might have come to this country and to these hills in search of freedom, but we brought in our baggage the innate hunger of the human race for hierarchy.

Go about thirty miles down the road toward Beulahville and you're out of the hills and knocking on the door to the Bluegrass. Beulahville is older than Blue Valley and truly southern. It had a slave market. Since before the Civil War, Pascal's family have been the Farnsworths of that town. When he was taking his meals at Mrs. Johnson's, his mother hadn't been dead long. Everybody said that he would get married after she died but so far he hadn't. Mrs. Johnson used to slip him extra slices of cake to take back to his rented room since, bless his heart, she said, there was nobody else to see that he got enough to eat. She didn't do that for anybody else. He was too handsome to live—that smooth, long face with the wing of raven hair brushing the forehead—and he was the one who started calling Ruth "Honey."

Pascal would teach high school civics all week—he was a good teacher—and then on Friday evening board the six o'clock train for Beulahville. He owned the old homeplace; his brother traveled for some corporation based in Mobile and never came to town. At the station Pascal would be met by an old family servant. Moses had snow-white hair and skin that was grayish black, like an old inner tube. He would already have the sugar and ice and lemons and whiskey ready at the Dupre mansion, and the drapes closed. On Sunday evening he would pour Pascal back on the train, whose conductor would in turn decant him into a taxi when they reached Blue Valley. Pascal was always on time for class on Monday morning, trembling with steadiness like a drawn bowstring. Sometime during the weekend Moses would have gotten control of his clothes. Pascal only bothered with two suits and two ties and one pair of shoes at a time, all very expensive. He had a winter suit and tie and a summer suit and tie. Moses would put a crease in the trousers that you could slice bread with and shine up the tan shoes until it seemed in the Sunday twilight that Pascal was wearing light bulbs on his stumbling feet to light his way off the train.

One particular Sunday evening, shortly after Honey had moved into the apartment at Mrs. Vestal's, she heard something scrabbling at the door. When she opened it there Pascal was, trying to smile but bent over like his ribs were broken. He looked so bad that she started to cry. He didn't have an explanation for being there and she didn't ask for one. She fed him chipped beef on toast and coffee and then she walked him home. It was hard to get a taxi after about nine o'clock in Blue Valley then; probably the one that brought Pascal to her had the sidewalks rolled up in the trunk. After the third time he turned up like that, she bought a little Ford so she could get him home in comfort. To this day he has never learned to drive.

One day not long after that, a substitute showed up to teach his classes and in that way we learned that he was going to spend the rest of the war playing piano in a USO band called Pascal Dupre and the Debonaires. He had a knock-down barroom style that supposedly he had learned at college. The sound of it made you want to throw away everything that mattered to you. On Sunday mornings he was on a radio program out of Louisville and Honey stopped going to church so she could hear him. People excused her; she was so lucky to have Pascal, that it was a small price to pay. It was while he was away that she got so fat, but when he came back they picked right up where they'd left off. Pascal seemed more settled. He made a garden and gave the neighbors cucumbers, bell peppers, tomatoes, and summer squash. From time to time he would stay in town for the weekend and he and Honey would have people to dinner in her apartment; or they would take Honey's landlady, Mrs. Vestal, for a drive in the country. Pascal was wonderful with old ladies and he knew all the points of local historical interest. It was about that time that Honey should have been promoted; but with all the canning of Pascal's vegetables and his interest in playing bridge and the other little entertainments he planned, she neglected her teaching for a few years. Every spring for twenty years they chaperoned the high school senior prom. On that evening he would wear his summer suit for the first time that year and Honey would wear her black taffeta dress, which for every prom would have to be let out a little more around the waist and under the arms. People said that she was good for him and that when Moses died, Pascal would marry her.

Two years ago we had a terrible ice storm in April. Coming down the outside stairs from her apartment, Honey fell and broke her hip in three places. Somebody phoned Pascal right away, but he never showed up at the hospital. Somehow his not doing so released some news into the air, namely that Moses had been dead for five years and that several times in the past decade, Pascal had been seen playing the piano late at night in Lexington bars with Delia Tabor hanging over him. Delia has been married three times and has a startling way of shoving her big bread-dough bosom at you to make a conversational point. So of course when Pascal finally got around to showing up at Honey's screen door with a pot of African violets, she quietly called from the couch that she wasn't home. He stood there a moment, then went away.

Honey took early retirement and went back home to Clayton Springs to live with her sister, who had had a mild stroke. Her Christmas cards say she's fine. If you telephone, she says she's fine but that she can't talk because she has to get back to her sister. However, people who have relatives over there say that her hip never fully healed and that she looks and moves like she's ten years older than she is.

Pascal Dupre is better looking than ever. He sold the Dupre mansion and bought a little house here, as well as quite an extensive new wardrobe. This spring he published a pamphlet about the Civil War soldier's ghost that haunts the barn on the old Tyler place. They sell it at all the gift shops. He doesn't drink now, because Adele Farnsworth, despite the difference in their ages, sees to it that he's not alone too much. In fact he's doing so well that people are saying it's a shame how Honey held him back all those years. They say she's lucky that she has a sister to take care of, so she won't just sit around and let her hip stiffen up.

The Man I Love

Interviewer: Thank you so much, Miss Susan Callicoat, for agreeing to be interviewed on this historic occasion.

Susan C: You're quite welcome.

Interviewer: I'm referring to your having reached a weight of four hundred and fifty pounds. You are now the fattest person in Moore County.

Susan C: Yes, at last.

Interviewer: You're pleased to be recognized for this accomplishment?

Susan C: I would have preferred to have some recognition eighteen months ago, when I finished reading all of the books in the public library. After all, that's not peanuts. But society has its priorities.

Interviewer: Well, in fact, this interview is for our library archives. Our librarian, your cousin Blanche Callicoat Long, has suggested that you might have some words of advice for young people wishing to follow in your footsteps.

Susan C: Wear sensible shoes.

Interviewer: Oh . . . Let's see, was this always a goal of yours, to be the fattest person in Moore County?

Susan C: No, it was not. Actually I don't have the natural talent for obesity that some people have—Tiny Whitaker, for instance, whom I just passed up. My metabolism is too fast. I have to eat thirty percent more than he does to gain the same amount of weight. It's hard, lonely work, I don't mind telling you.

Interviewer: But you have the desire. The heart of a champion.

Susan C: It's a combination of things. For example, you have to be careful about nerves. Many high school girls nowadays seem to have a great desire to be fat. They spend long hours training on Ho Hos and Doritos, but they're just too nervous to keep the weight on. I see them in the summer wearing those short shorts: little bitty bottoms, no matter what they do. I think of Shakespeare, "There's a divinity that shapes our ends, rough-hew them how we will."

Interviewer: What did you want to be when you were their age? A nurse? A teacher?

Susan C: I wanted to be an alcoholic.

Interviewer: I beg your pardon?

Susan C: However, as you know, Moore County is dry. I was held back in my early, formative years by this environment. By the time I got out in the world, it was too late to acquire the knack.

Interviewer: What makes you think you would have made a good alcoholic?

Susan C: A woman knows these things. I could have been the alcoholic equivalent of a twelve-hundred-pound person if I'd had half a chance.

Interviewer: You sound bitter.

Susan C: I am. Pass me that bag of potato chips.

Interviewer: Here you go. Miss Callicoat, could you recall just when you got the idea of being competitively obese? From these pictures, you were quite thin as a child.

Susan C: And that jar of mayonnaise, please.

Interviewer: Could you tell us something about your years away from Blue Valley? Mrs. Long suggested—

Susan C: That old liar.

Interviewer: I'm just saying, she suggested that—

Susan C: I refuse to discuss my personal life in any way. That was the rule you accepted before I agreed to do this interview.

Interviewer: I'm aware of that. But now I'm not sure how to proceed. . . . What do you think of liquid protein supplements?

Susan C: They're baloney. Reach me that six-pack of Hershey bars.

Interviewer: You're going to eat all of those too?

Susan C: Why? Would you care for one?

Interviewer: Well, maybe just a bite. I didn't have lunch.

Susan C: Sorry, you should have brought yourself a snack. That's the trouble with you amateurs; you never plan ahead. And another thing: amateurs tend to rely on a single taste to take them to glory. Your chocoholics, your peanut butter freaks. They burn out before they can bulk up. My method is to alternate sweet and salty foods, so that I can go on stuffing myself for hours without the taste buds blanking out and boredom ensuing. About a third of a bag of potato chips dipped one by one in mayonnaise, then one Hershey bar, then another round of chips, and so on.

Interviewer: I see. Well, unless you have any more advice, I want to thank you—

Susan C: You're not much of an interviewer, are you?

Interviewer: I'm with the Friends of the Library. Mrs. Long asked me to do this as a personal favor.

Susan C: The coward.

Interviewer: She said you would be difficult.

Susan C: You're not asking any of the right questions.

Interviewer: What am I supposed to ask?

Susan C: Dreams tell a lot about a person. Chew on that.

Interviewer: Dreams?

Susan C: If you had any insight at all, you would ask me what I was dreaming the summer when I was twelve years old. My best friend was Maxie Stewart. That was the year we were horses. She was called Wildflower: a black horse, with a white mane and tail. I was a palomino named Silver Star.

Interviewer: Are horses your favorite animal?

Susan C: Not particularly. All twelve-year-old girls are horses. The year before, we'd been dinosaurs; but our brains were too small to adapt to winter and we had died in the first snowfall.

Interviewer: What would be a typical day for you as a horse?

Susan C: There was school to endure, of course. But outside of that, we ran and ran, side by side, all the livelong day. And we climbed trees.

Interviewer: As a horse you climbed trees?

Susan C: This is a dream, you tiny fool.

Interviewer: I'm sorry, excuse me.

Susan C: Mostly we ran along the Trail of the Lonesome Pine. It isn't on any map that adults use. But every neighborhood has another map, the one children carry in their heads. The Trail of the Lonesome Pine connected all the child landmarks in Blue Valley.

Every tree along the route was a lookout post, a fortress; a jungle aerie.

Interviewer: Was there, in fact, a Lonesome Pine?

Susan C: So densely needled, with a wide skirt of branches brushing the ground, that you could sit out a thunderstorm against its trunk and stay dry. So tall that one summer night it hooked the crescent moon. From the top you could smell all the suppers of Blue Valley cooking and know when it was time to go home. It was our grandfather. It stood at the edge of the forest.

[*Sound of rustling food wrappers; then Susan C. continues*]

For strangers who may someday hear this, from the top of the Lonesome Pine, the town looks like a medieval fiefdom. The Farnsworth mansion is our castle. The iron picket fence surrounding its city block of grounds is its moat. The town huddles around the fence like a village of serfs and freemen. The hills are the outermost walls of the kingdom, keeping the world—I am tempted to say, the real world—at bay. This is why Blue Valley is the perfect place to be a child. Childhood is medieval, you know. To a child, everything has its place in a great chain of being, and everything is true. Everything: because a child lives by faith. Of course, dark things lurk over the edge of the world, and they are true too.

Interviewer: Excuse me, but aren't you describing the ideal state of childhood? Many children experience a grimmer, a less ordered reality.

Susan C: Then they are not experiencing childhood. They've been robbed.

Interviewer: I used to play in Elliott Creek when I was a child.

Susan C: But we're not interviewing you, are we? Maxie and I loved the forest. The four seasons lived there. In summer the air was green and tasted of mint. In spring it wrapped us in shawls of dogwood and redbud, that streamed out behind us in the wind. In autumn, we wore capes of flame. We were so much a part of the forest that in the winter, our hooves left deer tracks in the snow. It belonged to us. No one else ever came there. Then the wrong Edith came to visit.

Interviewer: Who was the wrong Edith?

Susan C: I am now eating fried chicken. You can't neglect your protein. The right Edith was my mother's best friend. Growing up together, they were like Maxie and me, two halves of the same peach. Sometimes I went with my mother to see Edith when we were visiting my grandparents in Indian Springs. Edith had stayed there and married a local boy, Roy. She was plump and pale and sweet and always gave me ginger ale to drink. Roy showed a lot of gold when he grinned. He'd greet my mother and me the same way: "Howya doin', kiddo?" The summer in question, Roy had been dead two years. He'd died of a heart attack right across his desk at the Indian Springs Chevrolet dealership. We hadn't seen Edith since then. She had moved to Chattanooga.

I remember, that is, in my dream, I was sitting up in the maple tree by the front walk one afternoon, when a taxi pulled up.

[*Sound of forceful chewing*]

Interviewer: This was the wrong Edith?

Susan C: If you interrupt me again, I'm going to sit on you. A thin, deeply tanned woman got out of the taxi. She was made up like a magazine ad, wore a bright yellow linen suit, and had orange hair teased up in a stiff bouffant. The right Edith, I should say, had brown hair and no makeup. My mother came running out and they hugged and laughed and then they stepped back and looked each other up and down.

"What happened? This is not the Edith I know!" my mother exclaimed.

Edith squealed, "Oh, honey, I got me a new life: hostessing at Howard Johnson's! Yes! And I've been taking dance lessons too!"

I dropped out of the tree and the wrong Edith said, "So this is Susan now. Honey, you'll scramble your insides doing stuff like that."

"I'm not Susan. I'm Silver Star, the famous palomino," I said.

She said, "I used to ride a little horse when we lived up on Sockleg Creek. She wasn't much bigger than you."

"Nobody can ride me! I'm fierce!" I yelled.

"Susan," said my mother.

Edith said, "God, Marge, let's go in the house. I'm dying for a cigarette."

"When did you start smoking?" my mother cried.

"Lord, honey, it keeps you trim," Edith—

Interviewer: My gracious, I can't remember my dreams like this, in such detail!

Susan C: That's it. Give me the microphone.

[*Metallic noises; a gasp*]

There. At dinner they'd talk about the extraordinary things they'd been up to, like eating lunch twice at Francine's Restaurant, which my parents and I only did only on Mother's Day. Another day they bought hats. As a rule, my mother only bought one hat a year, at Easter. These butter mints, made by my neighbor Olivia Boggs, are exquisite.

One afternoon my mother went to get her hair done. She never missed her three thirty appointment on Thursdays. Eventually the Bon Ton Beauty Shop gave her a twenty-five-year plaque for perfect attendance. Edith stayed home, saying that there was only one person in the world she trusted her hair to and that was Raoul, in Chattanooga.

I was sprawled on my bed, reading comic books, when she appeared in my doorway. She braced her hands high on either side of the door frame and swayed back and forth, humming "Hernando's Hideaway" and moving her feet in tiny suggestions of dance steps. Sunlight from the hall window shone through her dress and I remember being shocked that she wasn't wearing a slip; I'd gotten the impression you could go to Hell for that.

"Hi," she said. "I hope you know that reading ruins your eyes. It makes you nearsighted and you get crow's-feet before your time." Then she ran her palms approvingly down her sides and said, "I hope you wear a girdle?"

I shook my head.

"I don't know where your mama's mind is at," Edith clucked. "A young girl can't start wearing a girdle too soon. Otherwise your muscles sag right from the beginning. By the time you're grown up, you're already dumpy. The boys won't like you." She left the doorway and in a moment returned holding something behind her back. "Here," she said, tossing it, "from me to you. I've only worn it once since I bought it. I've got plenty. Now scat and put it on. If you do, I'll tell you a secret."

I could feel my muscles sagging like ropes of molasses. I ran in the bathroom, shucked off my Bermuda shorts, wrestled on the panty girdle, and pulled the shorts back on. The girdle felt like wearing last year's bathing suit, only worse in the crotch.

When I came back Edith said, "See? Now you look and feel better. Here is the secret I promised: even Raoul wears one." She started swirling her hips again. "Of course, Roy loved me no matter what I weighed. Loved me? Listen: the man adored me. He absolutely worshiped the ground I walked on. And do you know what? I still see him sometimes. I'll be watching television at night and I'll feel something, a clamminess in the air, and there he'll be, standing across the den looking at me so sad and mournful with those Asking Eyes. And I know exactly what he wants. Come in the living room a minute."

In the living room I found that Edith had been going through the music in the piano bench. One of my new lesson books, *Gershwin Simplified,* lay open on the music rest.

"Roy wants to hear me sing. Play 'The Man I Love,' " she said around the cigarette she was lighting.

As I stumbled through it. Edith leaned over me, dribbling ash, and said, "One year Roy was in charge of organizing the Lions Club Follies. Nobody in Indian Springs knew I could sing anything but hymns. But that night I wore a low-cut, stretchy black sweater and a tiger-print skirt tight as Dick's hatband and slit up one side, and—start over, honey, and I'll show you how I sang it."

I started over and Edith sang in a low, husky voice, with cigarette smoke boiling out of her mouth, that someday he'd come along, the man I love, and he'd be big and strong, the man I love. . . .

I was twelve years old and I thought I would faint from the beauty. She lingered on the last note, drawing it out so rich and soft that I could feel it humming all over my skin. When it had died away she said, "I brought down the house. Literally brought it down! And afterwards, Bud Tubbs came up and whispered in my ear, 'Baby, that was smoky.' " She wriggled her shoulders. "It made Roy so mad. He could be insanely jealous. And guess what? Ronnie—that's my teacher at the dance studio—wants to hear me sing too. When I told him about the night I sang at the Follies he said, 'Mrs. DeHart, Sugar, you had the Lions by the tail.' He said that to me when we were mambo-ing. Do you know how to mambo?"

I said I didn't and she said, "Good Lord. Well, I'll teach you. Every woman should know how to type, play bridge, and do the

mambo. Otherwise you start life with three strikes against you."
She lit another cigarette and flicked at her hair with her red lac-
quered nails. Then she said, "Did I tell you that Ronnie and I won
second prize in the fox-trot, on Ladies' Night at the Bamboo Room?
Of course, we're just good friends, he's working his way through
college—he's the cutest thing!—but when we were walking back to
the table with our trophy he said, 'You are one hot mama, Mrs. D.
I'd like to get into your—'"

"Edith!" The screen door banged and there stood my mother,
looking half scalped in a tight new permanent.

Edith laughed and said, "What's the matter? Kids hear worse
than that in school."

"You should be ashamed of yourself! An innocent child!" my
mother cried.

"Susan's growing up. She ought to hear how the world really is,
and not have to learn the hard way, like I did in that damned
hostess job," Edith said.

"Not one more word," my mother snapped.

"Don't tell me what to do!" Edith shrieked, "you smug, fat
thing! Sitting in your perfect little house with your stupid husband
that won't say two words to me! Roy worshiped me! When I married him, I became queen of the world!"

"He made a pass at me the night before your wedding!" shouted
my mother.

"You liar! Shut up!"

"In the church vestibule!"

I ran for the door, the shouts pushing on my back like a big
hand.

Outside, a warm summer rain was falling. I ran up the street
under low, gray wool clouds, my hooves settling into an even rhythm
on the pavement. Big soft raindrops splatted on my face like kisses
as I swung onto the Trail of the Lonesome Pine that passed the
head of our street. As I ran I anticipated the damp coolness at its
base, the smells of wet earth and leaf mold, so much like my own
horsy smell. When at last I reached our secret entrance to the forest, I plunged into it, becoming invisible, and took the slippery
curving arc of our path. The rain was different in the woods. Cold

droplets snaked down my neck like slugs, and wisps of breeze whirled up from the ground, chilling my knees. But I charged on, leaping roots, dodging puddles. In a minute, I knew, I would be safe and calm, inside the Lonesome Pine. Then I saw something that made me stop.

Several yards to the right of the path lay the remains of a fire. A fallen tree trunk had been pulled over for a seat next to it. Beer bottles, an empty cigarette carton, waxed paper littered the ground around it. At first I thought that someone had been having a party there the night before. Then I saw that it was old, maybe several weeks old. Do you understand? People had been there but Maxie and I had never noticed. I walked over to take a closer look. Beside the log lay a twisted sanitary napkin. I stood there a long time, listening. Listening to noises I'd never heard in the forest before. Twigs snapping stealthily. Someone breathing behind me in the underbrush. For the first time, I was afraid of the forest. I was paralyzed. All of a sudden, I woke up. *I woke up,* do you hear? I ran to Maxie's. Not like I used to run, but clumsily. It took forever; I got a stitch in my side. It was the girdle, of course. You can't gallop in a girdle.

I told Maxie what I had seen and made her promise never to go into the woods again. I don't know whether she completely understood or not. We never spoke of it again, because the forest ceased to be an issue in our lives. I showed her my new girdle, you see. The next day, she had her mother buy her one. Then neither one of us could run worth a lick. Once we slowed down, everything changed. Our friends got girdles too. When Cindy Mauk passed out during geography, the school nurse discovered that she was wearing three of them, one on top of another. Suddenly, all the girls were crazy to have a grown-up shape. I don't need to tell you what that leads to.

[*Long pause*]

Interviewer: I—I'm sorry, but I feel like crying.

Susan C: It would bring tears to the eyes of a potato.

Interviewer: How did you feel about causing this girdle craze?

Susan C: I felt hungry. Night and day. I've been eating ever since. It's the only thing to do. Because in the forest, as I stood contemplating the violated area, I realized that up until that moment everything had been a beautiful dream. Everything: twelve precious years.

Interviewer: Do you miss the woods?

Susan C: I miss the woods every day of my life. But if I eat enough, sometimes I fall into a kind of reverie, in which I am still running there, wild and free, and the Lonesome Pine is still a friend. Do you mind if we bring this to a close? You're keeping me awake.

Interviewer: Of course. Well. Well, this has been most interesting. And I see you still have a whole pecan pie left.

Susan C: It's a gift from an admirer, a thin woman inside of whom is a fat woman, struggling to get out. I'll get to it later this afternoon.

Interviewer: May I ask, in closing, do you feel satisfied with the way your life has turned out?

Susan C: Absolutely. They haven't built the girdle that can hold me now.

Interviewer: Miss Callicoat, you stated some time ago that you planned to weigh five hundred pounds in time for the Fourth of July parade this year. Do you think you'll reach your goal?

Susan C: Piece of cake.

Thence West to the Place of Beginning

He would go back, somehow. The time to have stood firm was when they took Mom to the Home. He could see that now. If he just hadn't gotten scared and called up Dreama that day when Mom got so wild, they'd be on the farm yet, watching those Kieffer pears getting heavy, with the corn so high you couldn't see the mailbox. Talbot shifted his position and felt the aluminum lawn chair shiver as if it would fly apart, then hold firm against his considerable bulk. Or say he couldn't have managed, say they did have to take Mom to the Home. Why couldn't he have stayed on? He had never been afraid of anything in his life. He spat a rope of tobacco juice out over Dreama's neat lawn. He had to do something, but what? The postmark on Charley's letter was already ten days old and he hadn't done a thing. But somehow he would go back, and take Mom too.

The mailman waved as he passed down on the sidewalk. Talbot stood up. The sun had eased his rheumatism. He turned the corner of the house just in time to see Floyd pop out the front door on those bird legs of his, grab the mail, and hop back in the house. Talbot cursed. The mail was the only thing he had a chance at. Being in the back bedroom, he never got to the morning paper first. He went on inside, not really expecting anything. It wasn't time for the pension check, and Charley's was the only letter he'd received since he'd left the farm. Floyd lay on the davenette reading a circular, two unopened envelopes riding on his stomach. Talbot would have cut his tongue out before asking about them. He saw that Dreama had gotten Mom up from her nap and had her in the kitchen stringing beans.

"Here comes the Preacher," Mom sang out as he took a seat at the table. "Nurse, the Preacher's here."

"Is he," said Dreama, working at the stove.

"I ain't the Preacher," Talbot said for the hundredth time, and then to Dreama, "I believe she's putting on weight."

"I never will forget how she looked when we come for her at the Home," Dreama declared. "Hair tangled and them dirty finger-nails. I druther they take me out and shoot me as to end up there."

Mom hummed a tinny tune as her blue-veined hands flew among the beans. He was relieved she hadn't woke up in a weepy mood. He abominated a crying woman. Floyd padded in and made himself a sandwich out of a cold fried egg and a biscuit.

Dreama turned around to look as he reached under the sink for the bottle. "You trying to create a disturbance?"

"Oh, this is my medicine," Floyd said, winking at Talbot. "Gotta take care of m'asthma. Don't I, Mom? Mom!"

Mom raised her head and looked dreamily at Floyd and the glass he was holding out to her. "Why, yes, Floyd," she said, her voice trembling from disuse. "You be sure to take your medicine."

Talbot said, "Maybe I need some of that there medicine. My rheumatism's been awful bad lately."

Dreama flung the skillet down on the stove. "You two old coots is going to drive me to the funny farm!"

"Look-a-there," Floyd crowed. "She don't never forget who Floyd is. Do ye, Mom? We friends, ain't we, Mom?"

"Friends," said Mom, and laughed high and silver.

It was that long time in the afternoon. While he sat, Talbot sharpened Dreama's butcher knife and his penknife. Then he sat some more and it was still two hours till suppertime. He didn't remember the desk right off because he wasn't in the habit of thinking about it yet, but when he did he got right up and went to look at it.

It sat by the window in the utility room, as big and scarred as he was himself, right where the men had put it when they'd brought it yesterday. He'd always wanted a rolltop desk. Not that Dreama would have gone out and bought him one, he didn't flatter himself that much, but somebody she knew in an office had wanted to get rid of it for nothing and she had asked for it. She probably realized a man with his concerns couldn't set on the davenette all day long. He went to the bedroom and brought a straight-backed chair, almost sat down, then thought again and went back to the bedroom. From the tray of the trunk which contained everything they had brought from the farm, he took out his books and papers and carried them out to the utility room. In the shelf on top of the desk he set his schoolteaching books and the animal books that Norton and his family had lately been sending for Christmas and birthdays. Then he began to lay out his papers into the pigeonholes, feeling as he did so a nice sense of order. To the right, his teacher's certificate, long expired, and the bankbook. He wondered what Dreama would say if she knew he only had $100.36 in there. But he would change that. To the left, his receipts, his birth certificate and marriage license, and the deed to the farm. He hesitated over the deed, tempted to slip it to the neighbor Mrs. Barnes for safekeeping as he had done with the will. No: better to keep it close to him. He spread it out on the desk along with Charley's letter and put on his glasses. *The renters think they have got the place for good, says Charley, they don't think you're coming back. They said they could get it cheap and if you won't deal with them Dreama will. They want to tear the house down.*

beginning at a stone on Military Line being on South side on Nine Mile Creek, thus running east to a stone on Squire Bennet's land, thence north one-hundred (100) rods to a white oak corner

He wanted to take a pitchfork and clean the lot of them out of his house. He felt like jerking a tree out of the ground and sweeping their truck over the bank with it. What made him the maddest was that they thought he didn't count anymore, that they could get around him, just because Dreama had rented out the place in all the confusion of Mom's illness and him having that one dizzy spell. They were some trash from up the river and didn't have any idea how important he was: how everybody in the hollow would come to him for help with wills and deeds, how once he could beat any man alive working, in fact still could put in a good day. After all the years he had put in on that land, they thought they could come along and get hold of it with mere money.

> thence west to mouth of Nelson's branch, thence west to land of Hannah Nolan's land, thence with said line southwest to a stone on Ohio River turnpike.

Still, he couldn't think what to do.

That night when they went to bed Talbot moved Mom's pillow, and Floyd's cigarette lighter fell out. Back in the pillowcase he found Dreama's reading glasses, which had been lost since Monday, and the sugar spoon. When he took them away, Mom started a crying jag. Talbot lay in bed and thought about the farm. The old dream began to rear again in him, the dream of standing on the bridge across Nine Mile Creek and owning all the land as far as he could see in all directions. For a while, in the thirties, it had seemed not only possible, but easy: a man of his sense and size, with two sons to help him, determined to beat the land and become something. Who would have thought Randall would have run to drink, finally to be lying dead in a pasture, and Norton be carried off by all those old fairy tales he was always reading into schoolteaching. That was Mom's influence: Mom always regretted not staying a schoolmarm. Teaching school had never been anything to him but a steady living, just some way to pass the time until he could think of how to make a lot of money. He'd had enough near misses on that score. Now Mom's boohooing beside him called up the sounds of the hoot owls on the ridge, the cats in the barn, the cooing of the doves under the farmhouse eaves. He wished he was home. Before she quit he was asleep.

He was surprised to find that the next day was Sunday. Since Floyd had gotten laid off there was no pattern to the week anymore. Being as it was Sunday, then, he shaved and put on a clean pair of overalls. After breakfast Floyd put one of Dreama's old hats on Mom and sat her down on the davenette. He turned the radio to the Gospel Hour and told Mom they were in church. When Mom got bored, Floyd took a nickel out of his pocket and gave it to her to hold. Then he passed his hat and told Mom to put the nickel in the collection plate. After that Mom smiled, but Floyd couldn't get her to sing. In fact all during Sunday dinner Mom didn't say a word, although Floyd said several times, "We been to church, ain't we, Mom?"

Talbot lay down after dinner just until Mom was asleep. Dreama had shut herself in the other bedroom with the Sunday paper, and Floyd was watching a ball game on television. Having the desk made Talbot feel good. As soon as he sat down at it, he began to feel more like his old self. After a while he thought of something to do. One by one he took down his books, drew a line through the old addresses, and wrote in his new one. In the *Key to Harvey's Grammar* he crossed out Gallia County, where he had started out, and McCurdy, his first school in West Virginia. The sixth reader had those plus the Riverview Hotel in Gallipolis, where he had taken a room for a year. Dreama and Norton had used that book, writing their names laboriously under his, and over in the back hid the name of Flora Baisdon, now dead. The fifth reader had the back off so he wrote above the table of contents

> Talbot Forrester Okey, O.
> Talbot Forrester Dunlow, W. Va.
> Talbot Forrester Greenbottom, W. Va.
> Talbot Forrester Catlettsburg, Ky.

and now

> Talbot Forrester Central City, O.

He'd not put the address for the farm near Blue Valley in any of them, although he had lived there longest of all. Because that was home: books didn't get lost when you were home. In the back of the bankbook he wrote, *Things Done at Dreama's. Set out 6 tomato plants by garage. Mowed lawn 2 times.* He waited a minute but nothing else came to mind. Yes: *Sharpened knives.* Then he wrote a letter to Emmie and told her about the little dog next door and the squirrels over on Alameda. It looked like Emmie would be the only grandchild. His name was written in water.

Through the door he suddenly caught Dreama's voice on the telephone.

"—Mom crazy and Dad mad as an old bear. Floyd laying on the davenette morning till night watching that noise on television and prices higher'n a cat's back. I tell you, I'm just paralyzed tired. . . . Well, sure he does. They all do: all those old people in the nursing home where we had Mom, they thought they'd get out. So he thinks this is just temporary and he'll get to go back to the farm. . . ."

Mom didn't say a word all the rest of that day or the next. On Tuesday morning during breakfast she said, "Phthisis: p-h-t-h-i-, thi; s-i-s, sis. Exhilarate: e-x, ex; h-i-l, zil; a, uh; r-a-t-e, rate."

"She's remembering those spelling bees before she was married," said Dreama.

Talbot said, "She could spell down just about anybody. I saw her spell down a lawyer from Ashland once."

"Whoo, I could spell good," Floyd declared.

"Spell *Floyd*," said Talbot.

"Now, you quit picking on Floyd!" Dreama shouted. "Just 'cause you was principal of a little old country school don't make you a expert!"

Talbot stood up so fast his chair fell over. "You shut your mouth," he growled and went out to the yard and broke the aluminum lawn chair into three pieces.

During the next week he went to the desk every day for an hour before dinner. He made out a letter to the nursery he'd been an agent for years before. Once he was back on the farm, he would need the money he could get from selling nursery stock. One morning he figured up how much he would need in seed and fertilizer and wrote it out neatly on the back of a receipt. Then he would read the newspaper until dinnertime. On Friday, though, Dreama started stirring around with the vacuum cleaner, so he went out and cut the crabgrass back from the walk. It was women's work; he knew it. Besides, the blood ran to his head and made him feel dizzy when he stooped over. After half an hour he went for a walk to clear his head. The cement tired out his legs before long, but he kept going.

So it wasn't until after dinner that he went back to the desk for his glasses and found that all his things were gone.

Dreama was in the back bedroom plaiting Mom's hair. His books and papers lay in a jumble on top of the trunk.

"What do you mean getting into my things?" he demanded.

"I didn't look at any of that old stuff. I just moved it," Dreama flipped.

"Well, it's going back and you can stay out of my desk from now on!"

Dreama put down the hairbrush. She had that bull-stubborn look of Uncle Abner's. "*Your* desk. Since when is it *your* desk? I'll have you know it's Floyd's desk and he's going to be needing it pretty soon."

"What's Floyd need it for? To put his feet on? I've got to have that desk for my business."

"I seen what kind of business you're doing," Dreama said. "Working the crossword puzzle in the newspaper. Floyd's aiming to set up as a salesman and that desk is the start of it."

Talbot went toward her, not knowing what he was going to do. But Dreama wasn't even looking at him anymore. She raised Mom out of the chair and started with her out the other door. "Today's Mom's doctor appointment," she said. "We'll be back after a while."

From the side yard Talbot watched Floyd and Dreama and Mom drive off. When they had turned the corner he went to the fence and called softly.

"Ricky. Ricky. You out here?"

A scuttling in the leaves under the Barneses' porch told him Ricky was in his favorite hiding place.

"I'll give you a quarter if you'll do something for me."

The kid came out and sidled along the fence till he was even with Talbot. He raised his weak, bleached blue eyes to Talbot's face and waited.

"You remember that day I gave your mother a paper to keep for me," Talbot said carefully. "You remember?"

"Yes," said Ricky, looking like he didn't.

"It was folded longways and your Mama said she would put it in the Bible. Do you know where the Bible is, Scout?"

"Yes," looking more interested now.

"Well, she was just keeping that paper for me and I want it back now. Only, that will be a secret between you and me. Can you slip in like a Indian scout and get it for me?"

Ricky was kicking the fence methodically, knocking off chips of paint. "I don't know."

Talbot took the quarter out of his pocket and held it up. "I don't believe you can do it," he said. "I believe you're not a brave enough scout to slip in and rescue that paper without anyone seeing you."

"I can, too."

"Well, then do it. You can have the quarter when you get back."

Ricky was gone a long time. When he came back Talbot took the paper and handed over the quarter. He said, "And if you ever tell anybody about this I'll whale the living daylights out of you. Even if I'm not here I'll find out and come back after you." Then he took his last will and testament around to the incinerator and burned it.

He was waiting on the porch when Floyd got back and was in the car with his suitcase before Floyd could switch off the motor. "When you got to pick up Mom and Dreama?"

"Four." Floyd was looking at him bug-eyed, with his ears laid back.

"Take me to the bank."

When he had the $100.36 in his wallet, he made Floyd take him to the bus station. That was the only time he almost weakened, when he got out of the car and said to Floyd, "You tell Mom—Sarah—not to worry." It was saying *Sarah* that almost broke him. He hadn't called her that for months.

Because he left without consulting schedules, just taking the first bus toward Blue Valley, he ran into a four-hour layover and a milk run that stopped at every wide place in the road. So it wasn't till five o'clock the next morning that he stepped off below Preacher Verble's and knew he was home. For a moment he stood still, breathing the bus fumes mixed with cold country air and letting the joggling subside in his bones. Then he started walking up the hollow.

The farm rose out of the mist to meet him, gray, solid, eternal, the house gathering the other buildings to her. How many mornings had he gone out in this fog to do the milking. . . . In fact, it was hard to believe he was not doing that now, that he couldn't go right into the barn and put the stool down beside old Elsie. He stopped across the road from the place. A poorly fed hound dog started out but slinked back when he chucked a rock at it. Although he had never been one to prettify a place and trim every blade of grass the way Norton did, it hurt him to see the tangles of barbed wire snarling around the yard and such a sickly little garden with the tomatoes not even staked. Parts of three or four old cars were pulled up around the barn so you couldn't even get in the door. After a while he came to and realized he'd been staring at the bank of pink on the fence, Mom's sweet peas, and planning his morning like he used to while he milked. They weren't going to make it, the renters: too shiftless. He was glad because that would make it even easier to get rid of them. He turned away and continued up the hollow toward Charley's, telling himself they'd have to get up mighty early in the morning to beat old Talbot.

When he got there, Charley had just come in from milking and Mrs. Carruthers was dishing up a larruping breakfast of biscuits and fatback. They weren't ones to show their feelings but he knew they were glad to see him and he knew he was glad to be there.

"Lord, it seems like you been gone forever," Charley declared.

"Only a few months," said Talbot, "but this morning when I saw the farm, it put me in mind of old Rip Van Winkle."

"Lord, Mr. Forrester, you always was long-thoughted," Mrs. Carruthers said. "Here, just set right down and have breakfast with us."

Talbot took out a five-dollar bill and laid it on the table. "I was hoping you'd let me rent Clum's old room for a while," he said. "Room and board by the week."

"We couldn't take money," said Charley, "but you're welcome to whatever we've got."

"No," said Talbot, "I'm here on business and I'd like to treat this as business too."

He'd meant to catch the renters at noon, when the man was in from the fields, but he lay down in Clum's room after breakfast for a nap and didn't wake up until two. Mrs. Carruthers had saved dinner for him.

She waited until he was on the pie before she asked, "How's Sarah, Mr. Forrester?"

"She'll be all right as soon as I get her back here," Talbot said. "She had a bad spell back there but she'll be all right once she gets home. She don't know where she is now."

"I'd druther die right here in my own bed," said Mrs. Carruthers. "My brother Ralph says he likes it in Lexington but he's mighty quick to come home of a summer and get some decent food."

Now that he was home he found there was no need to hurry. He chopped kindling for Mrs. Carruthers till supper and then swapped yarns with Charley until bedtime. But the next afternoon, Sunday, he walked down to the farm. The renter was sitting in his, Talbot's, chair under the maples, with his wife next to him on a crate. They didn't say a word when he walked in the gate.

"Howdy," said Talbot, pulling up the other chair and sitting down.

"Say, you're Mr. Forrester, ain't you?" whined the man. "What can I do fer ye? Ain't your daughter been getting the rent?"

"She's getting it," said Talbot. "Everything going all right around here?"

The wife touched the man on the sleeve and withdrew her hand to clutch her dress together at her neck. She was chicken-breasted and thin.

"Well," the man began, "my wife's not too pert lately and she suffers something awful on a cold night. I was wondering if you could fix the bedroom so's it won't be so drafty. And they's some boards loose on the back porch which a feller could break his neck out there in the dark."

Talbot felt a tightening through his chest but he spoke calmly. "I wouldn't worry about any of that. What I came to tell you is that I'm moving back here and you'll have to find somewhere else to live."

It surprised them, all right. In fact it more than surprised them: there was something else hiding behind their eyes. He took a deep breath and guessed. "How much you folks been offered for this place?"

"We ain't been offered. We was going to offer you," the woman said.

"Get in the house!" screamed the man.

"She didn't do any harm," Talbot said. "I suspicioned something when I heard about you wanting to buy. I knew from your looks that you didn't have the money. So you had to be hoping to buy cheap and sell dear. You might as well tell me. You're not going to get to do it anyhow. I guess you thought you could put one over on my daughter." The renter looked at his wife. Finally he said, "Feller wants to put in a subdivision." Talbot stood up, trembling. "We'll see about that. I'm giving you folks a week from today to clear out. I'll be needing to put in a fall garden pretty soon." "Place is too big for one man," the renter said sullenly. "I notice it's too big for you," Talbot rejoined.

By the time he got back out on the road he was shaking with anger, thinking about bulldozers and crackerbox houses and cheap-jack grocery stores being built on his land. It would change everything in the hollow. If a subdivision went in, it would be just like living at Dreama's. But he had saved them. He had always been the one people looked to for advice, and now he had stepped in again and kept away what would ruin them. He had started out to save himself and Mom and he had ended up saving everybody.

When he got to Charley's he helloed in the door but decided not to go in until he cooled off from the walk and the banging in his chest settled down. He sat back in the shade on the porch with his legs a little in the sun and looked off down the green burning hillside toward his land beginning at two beeches on the Military Line on the Ohio River Hill just past the school his three children had gone to, thence N. seven (7) degrees and 45 minutes, W. fifty-four (54) rods to a stake near where Norton had gotten the ax tangled in wild grapevines and cut his foot, coming home to take off his shoe in the kitchen so that the blood poured out in a dark pool over the linoleum, from which a sugar tree marked as side line bears S. sixteen (16) degrees and 30 minutes, E. twenty (20) feet through the Round Bottom where the violets made a purple carpet every spring and Randall let the mule run into the creek with him when he was too young to hold him, from which stake a large rock in said creek bears N. 82 degrees, E. ten (10) feet, S. 33 degrees whence he could hear the dinner bell at noontime and just see Sarah standing in the yard, her white apron a bright butterfly poised on his land. And then somehow he was not in the chair but lying face down on the floorboards as behind him Mrs. Carruthers screamed and screamed; and as Charley's rough hands turned him over he thought that maybe he had not done everything he had wanted in life, but at least he had kept himself from being buried in foreign soil.

Blanche Long Sees How Buddy Crosley Got Where He Is Today

Since Buddy Crosley has been in the news so much lately, people have been comparing notes on him and recalling his past, so as to make up their minds what to do. Nothing new has surfaced, not after all this time in a place like Blue Valley, which is so small that you know even the people you don't know. It's just been a matter of putting the whole picture together.

Buddy grew up on Tackett Avenue, which then, as now, was four blocks of frame houses with old-fashioned flowering shrubbery scattered about the small front yards, lilac, spirea, rose of Sharon, and blue hydrangea. His father was a traveling salesman and his mother worked at the jewelry store. Two undistinguished older brothers had after-school jobs and drove a green car. If there were five people sitting in a restaurant and they were two of them, you would only be able to remember the other three. The first time anybody really noticed Buddy was the summer he figured out how to take advantage of the sidewalk traffic. This was in the calm Eisenhower years, when men went off to work every morning and most women stayed home, raising their children, hanging out the wash, and making jelly. The town was even smaller then, no parking lots and no suburbs. Many people walked to and from work, often coming home for the noon meal, and lots of women were out pushing strollers or doing the shopping on foot.

One day when Buddy was about ten years old, he set up a card table in his front yard and on the table arranged four piles of rocks, each with a label:

DIMONDS   GOLD OR   QWARTZ   MAGIC ROCKS

5 CENTS EACH

That was the summer the new community pool was dedicated, and every other boy in town was in the water from the minute it opened until it closed at night. But there sat Buddy with his rocks, which made people realize that although he was one of the regulars in all the Tackett Avenue softball and kick-the-can games, if he didn't show up nobody went looking for him. He was just a quiet, fat kid who was usually chosen somewhere past the middle of the group when playground team captains selected their players. But whereas his brothers never even noticed their anonymity, Buddy seemed to yearn silently for an identity, any identity. Possibly this need led to his exchange with Miss Portia Sophia Jefferson when she passed by Buddy's table one bright August morning. Miss Jefferson does not approve of children and has never acknowledged that she ever was one. But Buddy called out with a great deal of poise, "That certainly is a pretty suit, Miss Jefferson. How about a nice diamond to go with it?" and she stopped and stared at him. Most children ran when they saw her coming down the street.

"And just where did you get these treasures, young man?" she demanded.

"From the driveway," Buddy said promptly.

Miss Jefferson widened her eyes to terrify him, the way she did with hapless children who tried to sell charity candy at her door. "Why should I buy anything from you?" she barked, beginning to enjoy herself.

Instead of running away, Buddy merely sighed and let his shoulders slump. "I'm gonna let you in on something, Miss Jefferson," he said. "I was in the lemonade business two summers and it's a mess. You got to buy lemons and sugar and paper cups. Then you got to get ice and a pitcher from your mother and mix it all up. Plus you get yellow jackets buzzing around. And you know what? People don't buy the lemonade 'cause they're thirsty. I watch them.

Like Mr. Duncan always walks off with a cup like he's drinking it? Then he pours it in Mrs. West's hedge. They buy it 'cause they feel sorry for a little kid. So I figure, why go to all that trouble? As long as they don't want what you're selling anyway, why not just make it rocks? That way you get a clear profit. Everybody'll be sorry they didn't go into business with me," he concluded with modest sorrow, then shrugged and began to straighten his pebbles. Looking over her shoulder to be sure no one was looking, Miss Jefferson quickly bought three diamonds and two magic rocks. Of course, in Blue Valley someone is always looking. By the end of the day, everybody in town had heard the story and a bunch of them had bought a rock or two.

Since Armistice had not been declared in the comic books or the movies, Buddy and his friends spent a good part of growing up fighting World War II. One afternoon they threw firecrackers down the sewer gratings on Tackett Avenue, whereupon the sewer gas combusted in a tremendous explosion that blew the manhole covers off and allowed them to run down the street shouting, "The Germans have landed!" Scrambling pudgily to get away, Buddy was caught and set down in a patrol car for ten minutes, where he wet his pants and told the other boys' names. For a week nobody would speak to him, until Trace Calhoun decided that being apprehended by the police counted as torture and Buddy couldn't be blamed for "squealing" when nobody had thought to provide him with a serial number to repeat.

He surfaced twice during high school, once as manager of the football team for a season and again for several weekends one May, when for cheating on an English test he was forced to mow the lawn of his teacher, Miss Opal Gragg. Sometime during the high school years, his father stopped coming home.

To people's surprise, unlike his brothers, who had gone straight to work after high school, one as a telephone lineman and the other cutting keys in the hardware store, Buddy went away to college, using money from his paper route. Most kids here go to Blue Valley College, if at all. He picked a small fundamentalist school in Arkansas for its short-statured football team, figuring that he had a better chance of being manager of a short team than a big, tall one; and although he soon learned he lacked the right local connections ever to be manager, he did become chaplain of the team after being ordained as a minister in his sophomore year. Ordination there did not require seminary study, but only good character and good intentions; and it was Buddy's intention to be team chaplain. This was right after he married a tiny sacred-music major from Blytheville. He was the first of his old crowd to marry and the first to divorce, a year later. The girl decided to join a touring company of *Hair* and told Buddy he was too much of a drag to be part of the Age of Aquarius. When he came home for Christmas that year he had an older man's low-slung paunch and receding hairline and wore pastel polyester suits even to play pickup games of basketball with his friends, carefully removing the suit coat but not his white patent leather street shoes. People recognized the bruised look in his eyes from his solitary rock-selling days, but he never said a word against the Blytheville girl.

For unknown reasons he left college without a degree and became pastor of a church in a flat, windswept town in Oklahoma. Within three months he and the daughter of a well-to-do farmer were married and seven months later they had their first child, widely announced as premature. With those obligations he of course did not have to go to Vietnam.

Nobody heard from Buddy for the next few years. Then one spring Doc Burns and his family went to Hawaii for Easter. When he took his kids in a Burger King on Waikiki Beach, there stood Buddy next to the napkins and straws. Thin, tan, wearing a Hawaiian shirt and tinted aviator glasses, he was managing the place. The Oklahoma congregation had found out about his college divorce. With a high, metallic laugh that chilled Doc Burns, who remembered Buddy as a sweet, if slightly stupid paperboy, Buddy said that instead of feeding the five thousand on loaves and fishes, he was feeding Whoppers to the five billion.

When Buddy came home for his mother's funeral three years later, however, it was not from Hawaii, but from Knoxville, Tennessee, where he had just flunked out of night law school. The Oklahoma wife's name was Doreen, and she was a lovely, fresh-faced blond of the ingenue type that on soap operas is always named Cricket. She was a shopaholic. Nobody will ever know how Buddy afforded her bills at the best stores in Lexington as well as the price of the first house built in Harborview Estates, Blue Valley's first suburb, which overlooks the borrow pit off the Interstate exchange. Some people say he made a killing in Knoxville, betting on SEC games. They and their three children settled in here—the youngest girl looked pure Hawaiian—and Buddy got a night job at the power plant. Days he commuted to embalming school in Lexington, and after he got his license he went to work for Litchfield Funeral Home. Some people said, of course it was just a rumor, that it was Mr. Mayhall, the jeweler his mother worked for, who convinced Buddy to become a mortician. Something about a business arrangement between Mr. Mayhall and old Mr. Litchfield which the jeweler wanted to continue. People sentimentally bury a lot of good jewelry with their loved ones.

One of the first jobs Buddy had was to go down to Beulahville and bring a body back. A paper in the wallet of the man, who had died of cirrhosis in a Salvation Army rooming house, said to contact the mayor of Blue Valley in case of emergency. The derelict turned out to be Buddy's father. Later, the clerk there said that when Buddy realized who the man was, he turned, walked downstairs, and went across the street to the drugstore. In a minute he came back with a pack of cigarettes and sat down on the rooming house steps. Silently he smoked three cigarettes down to the filters, threw the rest of the pack in a trash can, and went back upstairs to get about his business. No one has ever seen him smoke before or since. At the visitation everyone said Buddy did a beautiful job on his daddy.

When Mr. Litchfield retired several years later, Buddy managed to buy the business. Possibly some of his friends in Rotary helped him. His years leading hymns as a minister made him a natural for Rotary song leader, and he was responsible for expanding the repertoire of the after-lunch group sings so that they didn't ever have to sing "Edelweiss" again. After Buddy sold the extra lots he had gotten hold of in Harborview Estates before anybody realized that the town would have to expand in that direction, he built the new Crosley-Litchfield Funeral Chapel out on Highway 60. Long and low, built of red brick with a Georgian facade, it looks like an expensive private school. Unfortunately, the week of the Chapel open house, his wife, Doreen, ran away. Buddy and Sheriff Tompkins caught up with her in a motel in Chattanooga, in bed with two men, one a college student and the other a groundskeeper at the funeral home. This was on a Saturday night. When Buddy brought her back he also brought a new tandem bicycle unassembled in the trunk of his Lincoln. By noon Sunday he had the bicycle put together and had Doreen sobered up. For the next six hours he forced her to pedal all over town with him—they wore matching powder-blue jogging suits—to show that they were still together and there was nothing wrong with their marriage. Except for the drinking and the buying sprees, Doreen has never given him another bit of trouble. What does he really think of her? Nobody has ever known what Buddy really thinks about anything.

So things have turned out all right for Buddy, or as well as they ever turn out these days. Oh, there was some trouble about sewage backing up in those shoddy apartments he built on Meadowlawn, but he settled that out of court. He has sold the funeral parlor and is into nursing homes, which are the big thing now. That's how the Governor made his pile. All three of his children went to Blue Valley College for a while. The girl teaches aerobics in Albuquerque. The younger boy has a lawn mower distributorship here in town and goes through a custody battle with an ex-wife every so often. The older boy, who actually graduated, makes quite a bit of money in some kind of business that requires him to travel between Miami and Louisville. People don't like to ask; but when he came home for his parents' anniversary party, he brought a bodyguard.

So when the Republicans were looking around for a mayoral candidate this spring to run against Pop Fraley, who has traded the office back and forth with the Farnsworths since 1961, Buddy Crosley's name came up more times than anyone else's. People said they were tired of big names like the Farnsworths and the Fraleys. Those men are idealists, and while it's true that idealists will get you your statues and your parks and a decent school system and a hospital, the problems are different now, what with the collapse of values and all. Last week Buddy Crosley won the mayoral race in a landslide. People said that he doesn't have any illusions and that's what we need. He is the new breed. He's what's happening today.

The Art Business

The following events took place in the Year of the Pig, during the great folk art scare of the eighties. You remember those bizarre years, when the smell of potpourri lay heavy upon the land. Each fall, in time for holiday buying, a new stylized animal appeared on kitchen and bathroom accessories, dishes, clothing, wallpaper, and even furniture. Huge stores sprang up crammed with unpainted plywood cutouts of these totems, which people of normal intelligence bought and spent many weekend hours painting with pastel colors in their garages, in order to sell them on alternate weekends at craft fairs to others just like themselves, except that this second group did not have time to do the painting. If civilization had collapsed then, future archaeologists would have concluded from the ruins that the United States was a nation of small-animal worshipers: teddy bears, owls, symmetrically striped cats, bubblegum-pink pigs, ducks in blue bonnets, geese wearing little aprons. And of course there was that intriguing aberration in homage of the larger animals, the Year of the Holstein, with its proliferation of piebald sweatshirts.

By the mid-eighties, the folk art craze had even reached deep into the Kentucky hills, where I was living at the time in Blue Valley, the town that God mislaid. At my alma mater, Blue Valley College, where I had returned to take a job as secretary of the art department, the administration had gradually become concerned about the corruption of the indigenous mountain culture. Local music, for instance, which had once been a treasure house of early ballads from the British Isles and of narrative songs about regional history, had gone completely Nashville. Nearly every string band that played in the annual Mountain Heritage Festival included the obligatory three-year-old boy in spangled satin who could clog dance while playing "Rocky Top" on a fiddle the size of a pork chop. Finally the college president approached the local nobility for help. When I arrived back in town, an addition to the humanities building was being constructed to house the Tanner Museum of Primitive Folk Art, thanks to the generosity of Eldon Tanner, Jr., the president of the Tanner Shirt Company. His wife, Susi, had organized the Friends of the Museum, and his daughter Missy had just been installed as curator.

Then in her early twenties, Missy had been educated mostly in progressive private schools in the East. At one of them she had majored in art and had learned to paint clouds. She was not unprepared for such a specialty, as she had spent a good part of her life observing the sky while lying on her back working on her tan. Although some of her canvases did portray cloud formations, notably the (according to her résumé) "ambitious" *Cumulonimbus,* she had made her mark with a Boston showing of a series of monochromatic canvases completely devoid of detail, which modulated from the plain white *Winter Sky* through twenty-one gradations of gray to the blue-black *Starless Midnight.* This showing and her father's money qualified her to collect folk art for the new museum. The facts that I could breathe, type, and lift heavy objects with a great deal of difficulty qualified me to be her assistant. For long stretches of time there was little need for a departmental secretary, given the habits of the two people who composed the art faculty.

Miss Mona Temperly had studied art history in Germany, probably in Bismarck's day, and since the early sixties had been translating from the German a twelve-hundred-page, eighteenth-century rhymed treatise on aesthetics. She worked on an Underwood typewriter old enough to be her mother, wore the key to her filing cabinet around her neck, and was so shy that she sometimes flattened herself in recessed doorways to avoid being spoken to by her students.

Ted McKinney, the junior member of the department, only came to campus from his house five blocks away half a dozen times in a semester to check on the progress of his studio classes and to pick up his mail. From my undergraduate days I recalled that Ted had once been famous for a series of oil portraits of his wife, Arlette.

Then one summer a French housepainter came to town, why no one ever knew. While he was painting the McKinneys' house, he and Arlette fell in love. After they left town together in the Frenchman's little tin-can car, Ted went on a rampage and slashed up all his paintings, even the one hanging in the college library that featured Arlette as the Spirit of Learning. Then he made a huge bonfire in his backyard and burned up all his painting supplies, accidentally setting the neighboring trees on fire so that the fire department had to be called. Since that day he had not painted a stroke or done much teaching, preferring to work on his collection of Studebakers, grow dahlias, play the bassoon, and put on puppet shows for himself in the house that was still half pink and half gray from when the Frenchman had abandoned his job.

One rare morning when McKinney was in the office signing a stack of overdue grade sheets, Missy was bemoaning her lack of success to Miss Temperly and me.

"We're just not reaching the right people. We've put ads in the school paper and in the *News,* and the Friends of the Museum have asked *their* friends, but at this rate, when the museum opens we won't have diddly squat in *objets d'art.* The rural people are just not coming forward. There *has* to be some primitive art out there somewhere. I mean," Missy snapped open her compact and peered avidly into it, "Daddy says Moore County has a per capita income lower than that of three South American countries."

Miss Temperly ventured, "I sometimes visit the rural schools to give art appreciation talks. I could—"

"Bull." McKinney, a great gray bear of a man with Stalin's eyebrows, swung around. "You're not going about it right."

"Oh *really?*" Missy riposted. She didn't like Ted because he had never complimented her clothes. In fact if Missy were to meet the president of the United States, probably the first thing she would do would be to twirl around so he could admire her outfit.

"Why don't you ask at Tanner Shirt?" Ted inquired, and turned his back on us again.

Missy blinked at us. "Why, silly *me.*"

The next day Missy went to her father's factory and made announcements in the lunchroom, particularly asking for paintings and drawings, of which we had none so far. She even stayed to eat with a tableful of seamstresses, reporting later, "There's enough starch in their diets to stiffen every shirt Daddy makes, but they're very nice." Other Friends of the Museum spoke to their husbands' employees, and donations started trickling in. Once we made it clear that we did not want Elvis memorabilia unless it was locally made, we were in business. I carried it all down to the basement— worn quilts, honeysuckle baskets, hand-forged tools, lockets carved out of peach pits—and the Friends periodically declared it all Art, as a priest might bless a fleet of fishing vessels.

"But what we really need is a Living Legend," Missy fretted one noon, as she daintily tore a strip of crust from her grilled cheese sandwich and nibbled it. In places Blue Valley is narrow enough to throw a silver dollar across. Every day a five-minute walk took us from the campus on the northwestern valley wall to the center of downtown, where we ate lunch in the front window of the Southern Grill. Across the street, pig-shaped candles and pig-faced coffee mugs stared at us from windows of The Jolly Pink Pig Crafts 'n' Things, probably recognizing us for the sitting ducks we were.

"Yes," I agreed, "but there aren't any Living Legends out there. We would have found one by now."

Our dream was to locate a certain type of person to designate as a Living Legend: a genuine folk artist, someone who would be laboring in obscurity for the pure pleasure of creating and of keeping the old ways alive. Sometimes Missy and I imagined a beatific old woman with a crown of white braids, working away at an ancient loom in a log cabin, weaving coverlets from designs brought to this country by her great-grandmothers' great-grandmothers. Other times we envisioned a thin, taciturn man in overalls and rimless spectacles who made dulcimers by hand while his grandchildren played in the wood shavings around him. We needed people like that to have heartwarming articles written about them and to attract publicity to the museum.

Suddenly Missy sat up and said, "Would you look at *that*."

Toward us on the sidewalk came three people walking abreast. The woman, thin and ponytailed, looked edgy, as if, my mother would say, she had pinworms. Her eyes swept the street restlessly. Nearest the window limped a rough-looking character whom I took to be her husband, in overalls and a seed company cap. Between them, leaning on a tall, carven walking stick that Moses could have used to strike water from a rock, tottered a sweet-looking old man with a flowing white beard.

"*Yes,*" said Missy, and of course we were both thinking the same thing. The old man's walking stick belonged in our museum. The woman's eyes swept across Missy, jerked back, and held. She broke into a smile. Her teeth were ranged haphazardly in her mouth like badly shuffled playing cards.

"Why, that's one of the seamstresses I had lunch with. Let's go and speak to her," Missy said, and swept out, leaving me with the check. The little group halted at her wave, clearly mesmerized by the small, blond apparition. With her perpetual tan, Missy reminded me of a Florida Tinker Bell, right down to the jingle; for her many gold chains, rings, earrings, ankle bracelets, and wrist bracelets made her chime gently when she walked. The secretary of the English department claimed that the jewelry made Missy look like a "cortesian," a mild enough remark coming from a woman who herself resembled an overstuffed chintz armchair.

By the time I got outside, Missy was examining the walking stick from every angle as she talked earnestly to the old man. The stick was undeniably handsome, perhaps five feet of gleaming, muscular-looking wood around which, from top to bottom, coiled a woody vine that had grown naturally around the original sapling. The vine had been stripped of its bark and leaves and carved to look like a snake, with a fanged head and a pattern of scales over its entire length.

Missy presented me. The old man, his cheeks apple-red at the attention he was getting, introduced himself as Archibald Bridges, accompanied by his daughter Myra Sue and his son-in-law Tolliver.

"Wa-al, I don't know," he then resumed to Missy, "this old stick's been awful good to me. I don't know if I could get around without it."

"But to have it on permanent display in the Tanner Museum of Primitive Folk Art—just think. You'll be known as a regional artist and maybe even featured nationally. The editor of *Art Now* has been invited to our opening," Missy argued.

Myra Sue piped up, "Daddy, I reckon we could get you one of them aluminum canes over to the Hospital Supply."

Archibald Bridges slowly absorbed the idea. "Now why didn't I think of that? Ain't she handy as a pocket in a shirt?"

Myra Sue brayed a smile at her feet.

"Course," he went on, "I'm thinking them aluminum ones is right pricey."

"Your donation is fully tax deductible," Missy said quickly.

Bridges scratched around in his beard. "I ain't familiar with the notion."

"Oh, all right, I'll give you ten dollars for it."

Shaking his head, he shuffled forward.

"Fifteen."

The old man stopped.

"And if you've got any other carving, I'll buy that too."

"Nossir, this is the only thing I ever carven, except play-purties for my grandchildren," he allowed.

She let out a little squeak. "Could I see those?"

"Naw, them kids has done broke 'em up," Bridges allowed.

Tolliver shifted his tobacco from one cheek to the other and said in a rusty voice, "Myra Sue here says you're partial to drawing."

"Heavens, yes. We haven't been able to find any drawing or painting at all," Missy admitted.

"Tolliver, honey, you don't mean to bring up them old things Daddy does," said Myra Sue.

"It's drawing," Tolliver declared.

"Naw, it ain't," said old Archibald, hitching up his shoulders and blushing harder.

Missy's hand lighted on his arm like a butterfly. "Why, Mr. Bridges! Do you mean to tell me that carving isn't your only talent?"

Tolliver spat a neat stream of tobacco juice into the gutter. "Up home folks call him Drawing Bridges."

"He'd draw all day if we didn't watch him," put in Myra Sue.

"Aw now, it's not nothing, just something to do of an evening," Bridges protested, starting to move along, but Missy would not be denied. Clinging to his arm she walked with him, and by the end of the block had not only made him promise to bring her some drawings the next week, but also had secured possession of the cane.

The next week, Archibald Bridges met Missy by the courthouse and handed over two crayon drawings on butcher paper. That afternoon she ecstatically unrolled them on my desk. One looked like a desperately ugly hedgehog eating a piece of string. The other appeared to be a man drowning in a royal blue puddle while several horned monsters looked on.

Miss Temperly, returning from four hours at the microfilm machine in the library, her eyes as glazed as marzipan, murmured in passing, "Sehr schön, sehr kindlich."

Early in the new year the museum addition to the humanities building was finished and the Friends sent out invitations, arranged flowers, and otherwise made plans for a gala opening. Not only did the Lexington CBS affiliate call to say they were sending a camera, but Joseph Schnall, the editor of *Art Now*, telephoned to announce his imminent arrival by car.

Missy had studied with Professor Schnall at a girls' school in Maryland and told me that it had been like being alive in Michelangelo's day. Her plan was to have the great man meet the faculty and tour the museum privately that morning, so that he could make a few remarks at the evening gala. Accordingly she sent runners to the library and to the ranch house on Hargis Avenue to summon Miss Temperly and Ted McKinney. At eleven that morning, when the Tanner Coupe de Ville let out Missy, her mother, who was representing the Friends, and Professor Schnall, the three of us were lined up at the museum door like servants of the manor.

Mrs. Tanner bustled toward us on three-inch spike heels, her lush, Deep South voice flowing like butter slathered on hot bread. "Isn't this the most *fantastic* occasion you ever saw? Missy, come here and introduce everybody this instant. I declare, when I heard Joe Schnall was actually going to grace us with his presence, I nearly fell out dead!"

Professor Schnall sported a dark green polyester three-piece suit, a lime-green shirt, a bolo tie, and cowboy boots. His long hair, which he wore slicked straight back, had been ruffled up by the wind into a comb effect, so that as he strutted deliberately up the walk he looked like a big green rooster wearing horn-rims.

Missy announced, "This is Miss Temperly. She's writing a very big book. Joe's written three books. I'm sure you two will have a lot to talk about."

"Did you have a nice trip?" ventured Miss Temperly.

"On these roads? In the rental car from Hell?" snorted Schnall.

"And this is our secretary, Betty. She did a lot of work on the show. Joe put together a wonderful exhibit for the Reiker Gallery in Boston. He wrote a *marvelous* catalogue," said Missy.

I shook hands with Professor Schnall. It was like squeezing a clump of cold, cooked cabbage.

"And here is our star painter, Ted McKinney. Joe has a piece in the Guggenheim's traveling exhibit, Ted."

"What sort of stuff do you do?" Schnall barked.

"Little bread dough sculptures. I glue them to refrigerator magnets," said McKinney, staring him down.

"Well," said Mrs. Tanner, "I think art is just *too* fascinating. And this whole experience with the museum has been unbelievable, all the fun we had at our coffees. Someday I'm going to write a novel about it all. I swear I will!"

As we entered the museum, Schnall whipped out a microrecorder and began speaking into it. The pieces showed off well in the bright, airy rooms—much handwork from women, such as quilts, rag rugs, hand-embroidered poke bonnets, and the dog-hair weaving of one Granny Hawkins. The men were represented in sturdier mediums by carved animals, an end table painted with a Last Judgment scene that included painted blood running down the table legs, some ironwork, and Archibald Bridges's walking stick. But the *pièces de résistance* clearly were the drawings by Bridges, who had continued to bring Missy weekly samples of his work. The Friends had chosen several to be framed for the permanent collection.

"These were done by the sweetest old farmer," Missy explained. "Isn't he great? And he told me that he hasn't been drawing all that long."

"And the *remarkable* thing," put in Mrs. Tanner, "is that he might be illiterate. Isn't that just too fantastic? Isn't it a hoot? These are *real* country people." She pointed to a wobbly, nearly illegible "AB" in the corner of one drawing.

Schnall stepped forward and peered at a crayon drawing of a host of light blue stick figures with wings fighting a host of red stick figures with horns and tails, over the prostrate body of a white-bearded stick figure. "Extraordinary persistence of primitive good-

and-evil imagery in rural America," he murmured into his re-
corder, "technically undeveloped in the extreme but conceptually
sound. . . ." He passed on to another drawing featuring a little
boy fishing in a stream. The trees overhanging the water had purple trunks and trailing blue branches. In the stream several fish
were staring at the hook, which was baited with a red valentine
heart. Beside the boy on the bank sat a green creature with webbed
feet, strumming a banjo.

"Surrealism . . . *les couleurs fauves* . . ." droned Schnall, "a frog
representing the dark side of youth encroaching upon the pastoral
setting, the hooked heart clearly a symbol of the loss of innocence
suffered by rural Americans in Vietnam—" he broke off to stare at
Missy over the tops of his glasses. "I am eternally in your debt for
bringing Archibald Bridges to my attention, Sweetie. Where's a
phone? I need to call New York."

At the grand opening of the museum that night the cameras and
reporters rushed to fawn over the Blue Valley glitterati: the mayor,
college president, state senator, and wives thereof; Eldon Tanner,
the benefactor himself; and wealthy Adele Farnsworth, who was as
usual dressed entirely in purple and escorted by the local intellec-
tual, Pascal Dupre, said to be related on his mother's side to the
painter Gustave Moreau. Less remarked upon were the folk artists
themselves, as faded-looking as their old quilts and including Archibald Bridges, who wistfully stroked his walking stick in its display,
as if patting the hand of an incarcerated relative through prison
bars. Joseph Schnall spoke learnedly to anybody who would listen
and to some who wouldn't, while in the foyer a string band played
mountain music, Miss Temperly and I served "nonalcoholic moon-
shine," and Ted McKinney ate most of the country ham sandwiches.

The next month Schnall's article on the new museum appeared
in *Art Now* with a lengthy analysis of Mr. Bridges's drawings, and
soon the department was receiving inquiries from folk art enthusi-
asts far and wide who wanted to own an Archibald Bridges original. Then the inquiries stopped and we subsequently learned that
Bridges was selling his drawings as fast as he could produce them,
through his agent, Joseph Schnall. Missy was fit to be tied, but
there was nothing she could do. Schnall would not even return her
calls.

Since Archibald Bridges had cut the art department out of his career, we might never again have heard of him directly, had it not been for Miss Temperly's art appreciation talks in the rural schools. One spring afternoon she, Missy, and I were on hand when a busload of children from an outlying grade school arrived to tour the folk art museum, at her invitation. Despite Joseph Schnall's perfidy, Missy had relied heavily on his analyses of the exhibits in working up a spiel for tour groups. The children listened with a minimum of fidgeting until Missy got to the wall of Bridges drawings. Then a disturbance arose in the back of the pack. When the murmur was augmented by pushing and shoving, the teacher, a Mrs. Dunnock, held up her palm like a traffic cop and boomed, "Excuse me, Miss Tanner. It seems that some of our students have forgotten their manners. You, Hiram! If I hear one more word out of you, you may wait on the bus when we go to Dairy Queen. And that goes for the rest of you, too!"

As if Mrs. Dunnock had cast a spell on them, the children froze. One little girl looked as if she might cry. But as soon as Missy resumed, discussion broke out in the back again.

By means known only to grade school teachers, while appearing to remain as fixed as the Washington Monument, Mrs. Dunnock glided through her students until she was positioned directly behind the offenders. There was a squeak like a mouse being seized by a hawk, and the crowd parted to reveal her clutching the shoulder of a skinny, sandy-haired boy.

"Evidently Nathan knows more about art than Miss Tanner and Miss Temperly," Mrs. Dunnock declared broadly, like a stand-up comedian. "Nathan, suppose you take their place and tell us about these pictures."

Nathan, all angles and sway like a newborn calf, shook his head.

"He cain't! He don't know nothing!" shouted the boy named Hiram.

Nathan's cheeks flamed. "I do too know about them!"

"Liar!" another boy shouted.

Nathan set his jaw and pointed to Archibald Bridges's drawing of the string-eating hedgehog. "This is my dog Buck killing a copperhead. And this," he indicated the man drowning among horned monsters, "is Rambo coming up out of our cow pond the way he done to fool that helicopter in the movie."

"Oh, *really*?" Missy said.

Nathan nodded. "And this'n, with the boy fishing, that's me. I'm fishin' with a heart for bait because I like to eat fish so much. And the frog with the banjo, that the lady just said was evil or something, why, that's just old Kermit the Frog from Sesame Street."

Miss Temperly clutched the beads at her neck. "Are you acquainted with the artist?"

Nathan burst into tears. "He's my grandpa and he said not to tell. But I do all the work drawing them durned things and they won't even buy me a dirt bike. They said the microwave and the police scanner is for everybody to enjoy!"

At least Missy had the pleasure of sending Joseph Schnall a telegram about Nathan's confession. Due to Schnall's influence, Archibald Bridges disappeared from the world of high-stakes folk art without a breath of scandal. Schnall himself soon turned over the reviewing of shows in the hinterlands to a staff member and now sticks close to metropolitan areas. Meanwhile, the Bridges drawings in private collections continue to increase in value, partly due to his rumored death. But perhaps the strangest consequence of young Nathan's revelation has been that Ted McKinney regained his sense of humor and zest for painting. He says the child in him has been reawakened. Now, several years later, he is becoming well known for his gigantic, playful canvases, across which dahlias, puppets, bassoons, and vintage Studebakers cavort. The dog-hair weaving of Granny Hawkins has replaced the Bridges exhibit in the permanent collection of the Tanner museum, and downtown, two of the craft emporiums are now video stores and the other is a thrift shop. As for the serpentine walking stick that started all the fuss—it is now clear that our meeting with the Bridges trio at the Southern Grill was not accidental—the night after Nathan's confession, someone broke into the museum and stole it.

The Lesson

At night when Lena put her son to bed upstairs in the slanted room under the roof, he would ask her questions. He was five and named Irish. Lena was twenty.

When are we going home?

We are home. This is our home now.

Then where is Granny Ulvie?

You remember Granny Ulvie lives in town.

Will we ever see her again?

Of course we will. Someday.

Tell me about my daddy.

Your daddy was a rich man.

How rich?

He had his own truck. A big, black truck named Widowmaker. Once he drove clear to California in it.

Why don't he ever come to see us?

He drove over the edge of the world. Hush now, go to sleep. Caleb is your daddy now.

Then the boy would put the pillow over his head, so he couldn't hear the hoot owls in the woods. Living in the country scared him. It was too quiet everywhere, like something was waiting to get him. But the pillow was nice. It smelled like under Granny Ulvie's porch, where he had his playhouse. Granny Ulvie's scalp showed through her hair. It was pink and her hair was yellowish white. Her hands were rough and knobby and she wore flowered dresses that were faded almost white and were dirty in two circles over her big bosoms. Once, out in the yard, she got down on her knees and showed him how to whistle the doodlebugs out of their holes. All day long he and Granny Ulvie would be together. Then a car would stop and his mother would light down and it would be supper-time. On some nights a rusty red truck would pull up and his mother would leave again. When they came here he found out the truck belonged to Caleb Wooten, who was his daddy now. At Granny Ulvie's there was a little black-and-white TV but here the TV was busted.

Sometimes after the boy was in bed Lena would sit on the daven-port and look at the blank television screen, imagining what would be on now. Caleb was gone a lot at night with his dog, Buster. If he took the lantern it meant he was gone coon hunting. But most of the time she knew he went down to the Pit Stop at the crossroads. Sometimes he would eat dinner first and sometimes he would want it when he came in. The first meal she cooked for him, he threw on the floor because it wasn't fixed like he was used to.

Lena knew how to cook but Granny Ulvie had done most of the cooking, while Lena had gathered aluminum cans to sell to the recycler and later worked at the shirt factory. When she started they paid her below minimum wage because she was underage, and the first week she stitched her hand. She thought she would live and die a factory girl until Caleb.

Tell me about my daddy.
Your daddy was the smartest man in the world.
How smart is that?
He had the dictionary memorized. And he had books.
How many books?
More books than anybody in the world. Maybe a hundred.
Why can't he come to see us?
He's busy learning things. He lives in a library, up in the attic.
Can I feel your stomach?
Here. Touch here. Feel that bump?
It moved.
That was its leg.
Who is it?
I don't know yet. It will be your brother or sister.
It feels like a puppy.
Caleb was gone all day. If he was working for himself, down in the field called the round bottom, he took Buster. If he was work-ing for Mr. Pritchard, Buster stayed home. The farm was called the

old Forrester place. If they got behind on the rent, a man named Charley Carruthers came to see about it. Old man Forrester had dropped dead on Charley Carruthers's porch. The rent went to the daughter, a McDonald woman, in Ohio.

Besides the cooking and cleaning and washing, Lena was supposed to take care of the chickens and the garden. She was glad that Caleb's first wife had put in the garden before she died. The fresh vegetables would make a healthy baby. Granny Ulvie didn't have a garden, but she knew where to find wild mustard greens and dewberries and watercress in the woods beyond the railroad tracks.

Weeds had taken over since the first wife's death. One early morning Lena was untangling bindweed from the tomatoes when something peeped under her left hand, causing her to jump straight backwards from a crouch and land standing up. The chick had little blood dots on her head, like she'd been pecked by the mother hen. Lena figured it was because Nettie, as she came to be called, had a toe missing on one foot, which made her hop funny. Lena knew about the crowd shunning the different one. Every time she went to live with a new family and they put her in another school, it had happened to her. She took Nettie up to the house, washed off the blood, and dried her dew-soaked fuzz. Then she and Irish wrapped her in a dish towel and put her in a cardboard box on the back porch. After that, Nettie didn't want to go back to the henhouse. She hung around the back steps all day, pecking for bugs and taking dirt baths. Whenever Irish or Lena went to the outhouse or down to the creek, she hopped along behind. By the time she got her feathers, she would eat corn out of Irish's hand and would ride on his shoulder all the way around the yard.

Tell me about how you came to live with Granny Ulvie.

This woman I was staying with, we were driving to Louisa and she stopped at the East Side Grocery there in Blue Valley to get lunch. She got us two cans of Vi-eenies and crackers and two Nehi grape pops. And I asked for a banana.

Did she buy you one?

No, she said I wasn't grateful and shoved me out of the car. Then she drove away.

And Granny Ulvie—?

She saw me crying on the grocery steps that day. That night I slept across the street on the porch of an empty house. The next morning Granny Ulvie came back to the store to get some milk and some peppermint drops. She had an upset stomach. I was setting on the steps again, so she asked me to carry the sack for her. When we got to her house, she fixed me breakfast and asked me about myself. Then she let me stay.

What if we had to sleep on somebody's porch?

Why would we do that?

What if Caleb gets mad like that woman and makes us leave?

Hush that. We'll be all right. We got a real home now and we won't do nothing to lose it, will we?

But when she was by herself she feared they might make a misstep at any time. In the bedroom, hers and Caleb's, the chifforobe still held the first wife's clothes. Caleb would not let Lena empty a drawer for herself. When she asked him about it, he said he would see. She kept her things in two boxes against the wall and coveted a pair of black leather pumps in the bottom drawer of the chifforobe, the first wife's church shoes. Under the nightgowns she found four photographs: posed portraits of three young families and a picture of a young woman with a long nose and close-set eyes, wearing a nurse's uniform. These pictures were all that remained in the house of Caleb's four grown daughters. Caleb said they were mean as snakes and he had gotten rid of them. They did not look mean to Lena, and she wondered where they lived. Sometimes at night when Caleb and Buster were gone and the wind moaned and the house creaked, she wished some of them lived just down the road and would drop in of an evening. The nurse looked about her age. But she couldn't complain. Caleb had kept the promise he made because of the baby and married her two weeks after the first wife's funeral. They were married by a Holiness preacher over in Elf King, where his mother was buried. After the short wedding ceremony, he told Lena to get in the truck. Then he went into the graveyard beside the church and stood in front of his mother's grave and his shoulders shook.

One day when she and Irish were looking for stray eggs in the shackly old barn, they found something interesting. Or rather, as Irish pointed out later, Nettie found it by fluttering into a stall, where he went after her.

It was a toy, a simple little metal wagon, a box on four wheels with a shaft in front. Lena cleaned and oiled it. After lunch she made a little cloth harness from strips of feed sack, and by suppertime they had taught Nettie to pull the wagon a few feet. Practicing to show Caleb, Irish said, "Then he will like us for sure, won't he Mama?"

At first Caleb did like the trick. Grinning and nodding he said, "Hey. That's all right. That's okay." But then he frowned and jabbed a finger at Irish. "A chicken is the stupidest animal there is. It'll drown trying to drink the rain. Stands with its head throwed back and beak open, catching rain till it chokes."

But Nettie was smarter than any other chicken, Irish thought as he petted her tiny skull. They were teaching Nettie another trick, that Irish had thought of himself. She was going to be his alarm clock when he started school. By putting a trail of corn kernels up the stairs, they were trying to teach Nettie to go up to Irish's room of a morning. Nettie still slept on the back porch. They didn't have to worry about a varmint getting her because of Buster sleeping in the yard. While Caleb was down at the barn milking, his mother could let her in. Someday she would just need to open the door and Nettie would hurry straight up to Irish's room, not even needing the trail of corn. But for now, Mama had to carry her to the stairs and set her on the bottom steps and tap her finger on the step above, to show Nettie the way, and Irish had to sit on the top step and to call her.

Mama, when the baby comes, will Nettie still be my pet? Just mine?

Sure she will. We'll get the baby something else. What do you think he'd like?

I think he'd like a lizard. I could let him play with Nettie. But she'll still be mine, won't she?

Forever and ever.

How long do chickens live?

I don't know, honey. But Nettie will live a long time.

I love Nettie, Mama.

I do too.

As Lena got heavier, the air around the farm got lighter and cooler. Pumpkins swelled in the garden. One morning when she came down to the kitchen and looked out, frost silvered the grass.

She placed both hands on the small of her back and pressed herself into an arch. A dull ache throbbed deep under her palms. Soon, she thought. Soon.

Nettie waited at the door. Bending gingerly, Lena scooped her up and carried her through the house.

At the stairs she called softly, "Irish? I'm sending her up."

Irish took the pillow off his head, rolled over, and sat up. Today was the day they were going to try Nettie at coming up the stairs without the corn.

"Nettie. Nettie," he called, and listened. After a long time, he heard it faintly: scratch flutter . . . flutter flutter scratch . . .

"Oh, boy. Come on, Nettie."

. . . scratch . . . flutter tap tap . . .

"Up here, Nettie." He took the ear of corn from the nightstand and shelled a few kernels onto the quilt.

Downstairs, the kitchen door opened and shut.

Caleb set the pail of milk by the sink, washed his hands, and sat down at the table.

"Where's the boy?"

"He'll be along." Lena put a plate of biscuits and a platter of side meat in front of him. She poured coffee in his cup and in hers and sat down opposite him.

Caleb split three biscuits and spooned gravy over them. "He ought to help you more. Sissified little town boy."

"He's only five."

"He don't need to be babying that chicken, either."

"You're right fond of Buster," said Lena.

"A dog's different. A dog does its job. I won't feed an animal that don't."

"But Irish is just a child."

"He ought to get started on being a man. Time I was twelve, I was doing a man's work. I was strong as a by God ox." He laughed through a mouthful of food and held out his arm, bending and unbending the elbow to flex his muscles. "You don't know how strong I am. Don't have any idea."

"Oh, I know," said Lena, reaching for the fried apples.

Caleb's hand shot out and clamped her wrist.

"Hey," said Lena.

He laughed again. "Try to get away."

Lena tried to pull her arm back. His fingers pressed into her flesh like steel hooks.

"Quit. You're hurting me. Be nice," she said.

"Be nice," Caleb mocked her. "Be nice. Is that what you're teaching Irish? I want him on time for breakfast. You'll make a damn woman out of him, letting him sleep away the morning."

"He's awake."

"Then why ain't he down here?"

Lena looked away but it was too late. He'd read something in her eyes.

He let go of her arm and pushed his chair back. "I reckon I'll just see what's going on."

Upstairs, Irish hung over the foot of the bed, peering down the dark well of the stairs.

With a last flutter, Nettie hit the landing.

Irish scampered to pick her up. Nuzzling her neck, he brought her back to the bed. While she pecked at the corn, he lay on his side and stroked her feathers.

"Man, Nettie, you could be in a circus," he said.

The landing creaked and he looked up. A sickening wave of weakness swept over him.

Caleb stood there, tall as a tree.

When they passed through the kitchen Lena watched them from where she stood against the sink, holding her belly with both hands. Irish walked in front, barefoot and shirtless in a pair of cutoff jeans, his body so small and thin and white that Lena suddenly felt she had not been a good mother to him. His lips were tinged blue, as if he had been swimming on a cold day. He did not look at her, did not seem to know she was there. Caleb carried Nettie, and he did not look at her either.

Lena stepped to the door and watched them march out to the woodshed. Caleb put Nettie on the chopping block and held her down with a foot on her head. He gave instructions which Lena could not hear. Irish shook his head. Caleb cuffed him so hard that he fell backwards and sat down. When he got to his feet, Caleb gave the instructions again and Irish shook his head and Caleb knocked him down again. The second time Irish got up, Caleb grabbed him by the shoulder and pulled him over to the chopping block. He showed Irish how, while Nettie's head was pressed under Caleb's foot, to pull her body up sharply and break her neck. He placed Irish's hands on Nettie and held them there.

Rolling away from the door, Lena braced herself on the edge of the sink and vomited into it. She vomited until the dull ache in the small of her back turned to a blazing knot. While she was rinsing her mouth and splashing water on her face, Caleb came in and dropped Nettie's body on the drainboard.

Her voice came out a ragged whisper. "Where's Irish?"

"Run off." Caleb went back outside, got in his truck, and drove away.

Lena sank to her knees. Holding her stomach, she rocked slowly forwards and backwards.

Irish stayed in the apple tree in the backyard all morning. Straddling a fork high up in the leaves where nobody could see him, he laid his cheek against a smooth-rough limb and closed his eyes. After a while, he thought of something to do. First he made the ground around the base of the tree go away. Then the yard went away, then the house, and the outbuildings, and finally the fields and woods. The apple tree hung in blue sky. There was pure blue sky above him, around him, and under him. He sat in the apple tree and there wasn't anything else. He would live on apples forever. But that meant he would never see his mother again. He started to cry.

The back screen door opened and shut.

Irish caught his breath and hiccuped.

His mother stood on the back porch, shading her eyes and looking across the ravine that dropped off below the house. She was looking into the woods on the other side. Buster lay on the porch. When he saw she was carrying Caleb's twenty-two, he thumped his tail and got to his feet.

Lena looked down at Buster. "Good dog," she said, and slapped her leg several times, so that Buster followed her off the porch. Underneath the apple tree she stopped. Without looking up she said, "Don't you go out of the yard while I'm gone." Then she and Buster went down the bank and across the creek, Lena picking her way clumsily from stone to stone.

When they had disappeared into the trees, Irish climbed down and went in the house. Upstairs he crawled under his bed where it was cool and dark and the friendly dust bunnies lived. Soon he yawned. Crying always made him yawn.

The next thing he knew, his mother was coming up the stairs calling his name. In the center of the room the light on the floor had turned a deep gold; he must have slept into afternoon.

"Irish? Are you up here?"

He stirred, scattering the dust bunnies, and sneezed.

The bedsprings squealed as his mother sat down. Her feet were right in front of his face, the shoes caked with mud.

Tell me about my daddy.

Your daddy was a strong man.

How strong?

He could lift me over his head with one hand.

Stronger than Caleb Wooten?

I found something for you on my walk. Persimmons. Granny Ulvie showed me what they are.

Stronger than Caleb Wooten?

Don't get briggety with me. And get out from under the bed. You're not a baby.

When Caleb came home from Mr. Pritchard's, Irish was on the back porch, hiding outside the screen door.

Caleb sat down and unlaced his shoes. "Where's Irish?"

"He's around," Lena said from the stove.

"I want him eating dinner. That's part of the lesson," Caleb said.

Lena's voice hardened. "Irish! Get in here!"

Irish sidled inside and stood with his back to the wall, making himself as small as possible.

Caleb said to Lena, "Where in the hell's Buster? He didn't come out to meet me. I whistled and whistled for that sucker."

Lena turned the pone of cornbread onto a blue flowered plate and brought it to the table. She looked back toward the door and as her eyes swept around they caught Irish's eyes and held them just a moment; and in that moment, Irish knew.

"I haven't seen Buster since this morning," she said, and went back to frying the chicken.

To Die in Singapore

Dewayne

This morning when I sit down to breakfast Darlene says, "Well? How do you like it?"

I look down and there's words on my toast. The toast is brown but the words are white, meaning they were stamped down into the bread before Darlene toasted it. They say, HAVE A NICE DAY.

"It's this thing called a toast stamp. Me and Camille found them down at Big Lots. Isn't it cute?" she says.

I drink my juice and start on my eggs and she goes, "Well, thank you very much. I try to cheer you up and look what it gets me."

I put down my fork. "Darlene," I say, "next time you expect me to eat a goddamned cliché, I'll shove it up your ass."

"Oh ho, Mr. Big Words," she says, her fat sow face getting red.

I pick up my plate and slam it against the wall, where it breaks and the eggs run down. I stand up, knocking over my chair, and head for the door.

"You know what, Dewayne?" she screeches. "Ever since you got back from over there, you haven't been right in the head. Someday I'll find out why, you turkey butt!"

I doubt if she will. She won't even find out where I am right now, though probably she'll call work and get them looking for me too. The hell of it is, I'd like to talk things over with Darlene. I've changed on that. I really have. Anybody would change after what I've been through. It's just that whenever I get mad or crazy I take it out on her, like she does on me. I know I've got to turn that around, but first I need to get a handle on this thing about Randall. For the kids, if nothing else. Nobody can say I don't love my kids. In fact, maybe Donnie and Deanna'd be the ones to tell this whole mess to, if I could figure out how. Trouble is, kids don't believe nothing these days. Some kid at school told Donnie that we never landed on the moon. That it was all just Hollywood, done in a TV studio. Donnie said, "He got that right."

Thankfully they are interested in my experiences in the military. Like when they stayed home and I was stationed in Panama, where I learned all that Spanish bullshit. Hello is Buenos Dias and good-bye is Hasta Laredo. Or Thailand. Even Darlene likes to hear about the food and clothes over there. So I guess starting with the military stories would be one way to go at it. That is, this business I've never told anybody about. Which I keep asking myself: Why me?

It was on my last R and R before I came home, in Singapore during the first week of April of last year. Me and my buddies were looking for this address in an unfamiliar part of town, when we got tangled up in a street fair and parade, something honoring dead Chinese ancestors. Anyway, we got separated. I must have combed that crowd for an hour before I gave up and ducked into this little dark bar for a beer.

The bartender wouldn't weigh much more than Deanna, who's eleven. He reminded me of an ant.

"Any Americans come in here in the last hour?" I ask him.

"No Americans," he says. "Never Americans."

It's nearly dusk and the place is about half full. Now I've always noticed differences in people. Like for instance when you're some-place on vacation and the people look different from folks back home. Like this one time when we were driving through Minne-sota, people were big and blond. Big teeth. Big fingernails. "Those are Swedes," I informed Darlene. On things like that I'm a pretty noticeable guy. So I say to the bartender, "What about that man back there? That has to be an American."

He gets very still, like he's listening to something moving in the walls.

"Where is an American?" he says.

"Table right back there against the wall. The fellow with that big swollen cut over his eye. Dang if he don't look like he was rode hard and put up wet," I say. You never know what they'll understand.

"I do not see a man sitting at that table," says the bartender. "But sir, if you see him, it is behooving you to go and speak to him. You are surely seeing him for a reason. That table is reserved for the dead."

Randall

Naturally there's no telephone here. That makes sense, otherwise what's the point? You could call somebody to come and get you or have them send you a ticket to come home. Or you could just visit a while, which would be a big help. Not that they had a telephone at the farm back when I got here, or would now even after all these years. I'd have to call Lambert's store and have Curtis take a message out there. And not that I would have wanted to go home at first, even considering the circumstances. Norton and I used to spend half our lives scheming how to get out from under Dad's iron fist. I remember the one time he said he'd teach us not to slack off during the daylight hours, so he made us plant corn all night by the full moon. In the morning our hands were so swollen full of blood from bending over that we couldn't close them around a fork to eat breakfast. All the next week we talked about going to Ironton and making welders like Cousin Proctor. Then we heard there was work in the shipyards at Norfolk, but we fooled around too long and Norton up and got the pleurisy. By the time he was well it was too late for us. Dreama never schemed at all. One day we woke up and she was gone.

Over the big mirror behind the bar is a blue neon sign that says this is the China Moon Bar. How many years did it take me to figure out where it was? Most of the customers are Chinese, Indians, or Malays, jabbering away in their own language. However sometimes you get what they call Brits and Aussies, who might leave a newspaper behind. Once Dad walked behind me all the way to school, whipping me with a hickory switch to remind me to do my lessons. I don't have to be persuaded to read now. It's like liquor used to be for me. I can't get enough news, news of anything. Once during the Vietnam War three American soldiers came in and sat down right at the next table. I wanted so badly to hear about home, but all they talked about was poker and Vietnamese women. Being dead is so damned boring and lonely. You'd think they'd at least let us be with our own kind, but there are no others like me here. Somebody wants to keep us separate. Wonder what they're afraid of, what they think we might do if we all got together. Maybe we'd refuse to die. Norton's a loner. He'll do all right as a dead man, though he won't have anybody's grammar to correct. Anyway, I don't want to go home anymore. Too much would have changed. There's somewhere else I want to go, but I've been waiting for help.

It's funny, the whole time we were growing up we had to listen to Mom and Dad marveling over how smart Norton was from the time he was born. Mom kept a piece of paper in the Bible with all the questions he had asked before he was out of dresses. Do angels have beds? Do flies sneeze? Do owls ask their grandparents questions? What is the state tax commission? and on and on. I only asked one question that anybody remembered.

What is the wind?

The wind is God's breath, said Mom.

I have a different idea now, sitting here in Singapore.

Dewayne

The funny thing was, I thought I'd seen him before. I kept thinking I'd gone to school with him, but that was impossible because he was a lot younger than me, not much over twenty-five. Directly I got it: He was the spitting image of a guy named Elbert Ray Barber that used to play forward for Blue Valley High when I was playing for Bethel. Elbert Ray had a fadeaway jumper that would melt in your mouth. His daddy, Chester Barber, went to trial for stabbing a man to death. Everybody said that the man Chester killed was Elbert Ray's real daddy. The man was found in a field the day after he and Chester had been drinking and Chester had threatened him with a knife in front of several witnesses. That was six months before Elbert Ray was born. Chester was never convicted because the evidence was all circumstantial. But when Elbert Ray grew up, he turned out to be dark-haired, and big and rawboned as a mule. Chester was a short, fleshy man with blond hair, and Elbert Ray's mother was a little pale redhead. I could almost remember the murdered man's name, because every time Elbert Ray got another sports honor, the story would circulate again.

By that time I was to the table in back. The man stood up and held out his hand.

He said, *You doing all right today? I'm Randall Forrester.*

That was the name.

Randall

I was four years old when we moved from the rented cabin on Wilson Branch to the farm. Old Squire Bennett owned the land, as his father and grandfather had before him. There was a boundary stone they said had been put in place by a young surveyor named George Washington. We were already living on the farm when Dad decided to buy it. I was his favorite and he took me everywhere with him. On the night of the sale, he took me into the bedroom and shut the door. Norton and Dreama had to stay in the kitchen with Mom. He carried a kerosene lantern, a crowbar, and a big stick. *Stand back,* he said. Laying the lantern and stick down close to hand, he pried up one of the floorboards and then quickly took up the stick again. A metal box gleamed in the hole. Flowing over and around it, like sorghum over pancakes, was a nest of copperheads. To get at the money, Dad beat them off with the stick. Once the doctor told Dad that a big part of Mom's nerves was due to worrying about those snakes finding a chink to come through while we were sleeping, but Dad said that a fool and his money are soon parted and his choice of guards showed him to be no fool. After Mom's first collapse Norton killed the snakes, which was the start of the bad blood between him and Dad. When that peckerwood walked in the bar, I knew he was a Bennett by his sandy hair and jug ears.

Dewayne

I woke up in a room with a dead man once. It was something that happened in Bangkok. I took him by his hands and tried to make him sit up before I realized he wasn't just asleep. So when I shook hands with Randall Forrester, I knew it was no joke made up between him and the bartender. I'd like to've had a minute to get used to the idea, but this Randall was in a hurry. He said he had a theory to discuss and he'd been waiting for somebody to talk to since 1942. Besides, he needed a favor.

Randall

From the first moment I found myself here, I've felt a constant pull from Moore County. Until I get loose from whatever is holding onto me, I won't be able to rest. It's as if I got snagged between the shoulder blades when I was crawling through a barbed wire fence between life and death. And what I've figured out is, the snag is fame. After all, wasn't I known from one end of Moore County to the other for my good looks and physical strength, athletic feats, capacity for liquor, general popularity, and ability with the ladies? Not to mention my roadster and my reputation as a practical joker. Not to mention the ball game they're probably still talking about. That was what I was the most famous for, and it must be why Dewayne Bennett recognized me. Now that I think of it, there was a Bennett there, a Horace Bennett that might be this man's grandfather or great-uncle. We boys from the hollow were playing against the Ball-Playing Moores, a crackerjack team consisting of Dad's cousin Ernie Moore and his eight sons. The Moores had been beating every team in sight that summer so there was a sizable crowd on hand in the pasture below Preacher Tompkins's. I came to bat in the bottom of the ninth with two outs, the bases loaded, and the score 5 to 8 in favor of the Moores. I'd taken the measure of the pitcher, so just for fun I let it go to two strikes and three balls. Then I uncorked one and took off flying. When I slid into home plate, this Horace Bennett leaned over and tossed a five-dollar bill on my chest. He'd had ten riding on me. Not only did I save the game for us, but when Crit Moore came back with the ball, which had gone over the fence, he was also carrying a dead mink which the ball had killed down by the creek. I got four dollars for the skin. A legend in my own time, that's what I was. "O where have you been, Lord Randall my son / And where have you been, my handsome young man?" Time and again the old women would sing that mournful ballad for me. Lord Randall is how I was known.

Dewayne

My granddaddy Horace Bennett used to take me hunting for dewberries and watercress deep in the woods. Once he showed me ginseng. After a tramp we'd come back to his little house and sit in rockers and he'd tell me stories about his life, great stories that I could listen to all day. Such as once he told me about a baseball game he was in, where he not only saved the game with a homer, but the ball hit a mink down on the creek bank and killed it. When he went to live with Aunt Lil in Florida, he told that story down there and got everybody to call him Mink. I loved Papaw more than anybody, and even though he died when I was twelve, I remember so much about him that he's still with me, so to speak. Now this Randall has to tell me his theory that the reason he's stuck in this bar at the end of the world is that people still remember him so well, otherwise he'd be at rest. But not well enough remembered, according to him, or he'd be stuck in a more interesting place. He figures that presidents and kings get to live out their deaths in someplace like Yankee Stadium. So it gets me to wondering if my remembering Papaw so well is keeping him hanging around someplace uncomfortable, somewhere worse than Panama. Then I think, lots of people are remembered after they pass away, only maybe you can't see them and talk to them unless you have some connection to them, like me recognizing Randall because of that basketball player Elbert Ray Barber. Which gets me to thinking about all the empty seats a person passes by in a day: on buses, in movie theaters, on park benches, in your living room. . . .

I order another beer.

Randall

Up on the hill past his beehives Jess Hardin grew grapes, great luscious Concords that bent down the vines like clusters of big

purple toes. I liked the raw-blood aftertaste of new wine. Every
year when the new wine was ready, I'd find a chalk mark on the
north side of the mailbox post. Even though Noreece Corbett and
I were secretly married I was still living at home and Mom wouldn't
tolerate liquor. About once a month she'd make the rounds of the
property, looking for bottles Dad might have hidden in the hayloft
or in a hollow tree, which she'd smash against the big stone foun-
dation wall that kept the barn from tumbling down the hill. There
were several men at Jess's that night. One of them, Chester Barber,
got to waving a knife around and threatening to kill me over his
wife, but he couldn't prove a thing. Jess had to get his squirrel gun
to calm Chester down. I never knew anybody that enjoyed making
enemies as much as Chester, or a woman that liked to make friends
as well as his pretty little wife did. I forget her name; there were so
many of them. Sometime after midnight I started home over the
hills, eating a raw onion to cover up my liquor breath. At that time
I was working at Mr. Burns's dairy and had had some run-ins with
a big brindle bull named Smoke. I hated Smoke and Smoke hated
me, and as I went about my work he'd watch me with small evil
eyes that had red dots in the centers. Coming over the hills that
night I lost track of my feet until I was flowing over the ground, as
strong as a hundred men, an army surging over the dark slopes and
ravines to have it out once and for all with a man named Smoke
who looked like Dad, the host only stopping to arm itself with a
locust limb, before spilling over the fence and suddenly falling
headlong and rolling into a ball that became one man again, a
drunken man unable to find the limb in his hand as a mountain
roared toward him, a mountain with the monstrous hot breath of a
freight train, a black mountain darker than the night, which col-
lided with him in a small specific impact below his stomach like a
knife slitting a cloth-wrapped plum pudding, the steaming pudding bursting through the slit as the man was tossed up, up in the
sky, to join the constellations.

Dewayne

Him and his bullshit theories. If he was alive, I'd kick his butt so
hard it'd jar him all the way back to his great-grandparents. *Did you*

pick where you were born? he asks. *Did you pick what family you were born into?* "No," I say. *That's because life isn't fair,* he says. *But we're all counting on death to be fair, aren't we? Death is supposed to balance the books, isn't it? Either you reap what you sow, Heaven or Hell, right? or everybody gets nothing. And we're all counting on death to be a change from life, right?* "You better cut this shit out," I say. *But what if death is just like life, just more of the same?* he says. *There's no guarantee I've even got it figured right about fame. What if you might end up in the China Moon Bar, or you might end up sitting at the bottom of a trench three miles below the surface of the Pacific Ocean? And it was random, Dewayne, with no relation to how you lived your life*—"Shut up," I say. "Quit messing with my mind." *You're right,* he says. *That's the one thing none of us can afford to think: that death might be unfair.*

The way it ended in Singapore, I saw my buddies go by outside the window. By now I'm so freaked by my conversation with Randall that I rush out and drag them in, to see what they make of it all. When we come back, the table is empty.

But before that, he asked me to do the favor. He wanted me to find out who was remembering him and tell them to lay off. He mentioned the Forrester family and a woman whose maiden name was Noreece Corbett. And he told me a puzzling thing. He only finds himself in the China Moon Bar twice a year. The rest of the time he's no place, like when you're asleep but not dreaming. Generally it's around Easter and again around Halloween.

When I got out of the service early this year, me and Darlene bought a house between Blue Valley and Bethel, near the Aqua-Stream plant that stonewashes blue jeans, where Darlene works. As soon as we were settled, I went to the library in Blue Valley, which is the county seat and closer to Stonewall Hollow, where Randall was from. First I found Randall's obituary and picture in a 1942 *Blue Valley News*. That gave me a turn, all right. Then I looked up Forrester and Corbett in the all-county telephone directory. No soap. All gone. Then I looked up Bennett. There must be ten Bennett families in the area, but I only know who four of them are. Next thing I know, I'm into birth and marriage records and deeds and wills, hunting down Daddy and Mama's people and *taking notes.* I even took a note or two on Darlene's kin. A couple of months later, I start dropping by the courthouse after work and sitting with the whittlers, listening to the old times. They've not mentioned Randall yet, and I don't want to ask. The way I see it, it wouldn't be a fair test unless he's recollected naturally. Nevertheless, the more I hear about everybody, the more I want to know. As if they're all my people, everybody in Moore County. It's like I'm trying to get the total picture or something, which I must be losing my mind if I am. I mean, we're talking Dewayne T. Bennett here. Now the latest thing is I go out to the nursing home and set with people that don't have anybody to visit them. I feel like I'm responsible for them somehow. I worry a lot about loneliness, mine and everybody's. A secret volunteer. Darlene would laugh her eyes out if she knew and say I was getting soft in the head. Or think I was after the nurses. Or maybe she wouldn't. Jesus.

Randall

You are what you remember. You are what people remember about you. Otherwise what's the point?

Dewayne

So last week was the elections, the first Tuesday in November as always. I'm standing in the voting booth in Bethel when the elevator finally reaches the top floor in my brain. As soon as I'm done voting, I drive straight up to the Stonewall Hollow community, northeast of Blue Valley. The polling place there is in the church basement, probably the same church where Randall told me he set off fireworks during a hellfire-and-damnation sermon fifty years ago and caused half the congregation to be saved. However the rest of the hollow has been flattened into a subdivision. Anyway I casually walk up to the table where you get your ballot and give my name as Roger Forrester. The lady opens up her book and runs her finger down, Farley, Feeny, Ferrell, Fields, Forrester, I'm reading upside down right along with her.

Finally she says, "I'm sorry, but I don't find a Roger Forrester listed. Are you sure you're registered to vote here?"

"Isn't this precinct thirty-two?" I say.

"No, honey, this is precinct thirty-one. You'll be wanting to vote down at the Co-op on Hargis Road."

"Oh, I'm sorry to bother you," I say, and hightail it out of there, my heart ready to explode on account of what I've read.

Randall

Once there were these two Brits in here philosophizing. Matter and energy is all there is, they said, there isn't anything else in the universe. So I figure that if we're matter when we're alive, then I must be energy now. And during most of the year, when I'm no place, I think I know where I am. I'm with the others and we are the wind. I like to think that some of the time, I'm blowing over Moore County.

Dewayne

I've driven up here every day since Election Day. In the new part of the Pear Ridge Cemetery, somebody is experimenting with plastic tombstones. When you're going to your loved one's funeral, you can just throw it in the back of the station wagon and take it along, heat-stamped with the loved one's name. They have an opening in back so you can pour gravel in to weight the base. But Randall's grave is in the old part of the graveyard, on the lip of a hill overlooking the valley. I sit quietly a while, thinking about the fix we're all in. I think about how good it was between Darlene and me when we first met and I try to think how to get that back. Quit smashing my breakfast against the wall, for one thing. I think about my children growing old. Sometimes I try to recall everybody I've ever known, starting with the first grade, picturing each row in the classroom, and moving on up through high school and basic training and all through the military. Then I try to forget them all. Sometimes I think I'll go crazy trying to decide which would be better to do, to remember or to forget them. I also wonder whether I ought to look up Elbert Ray Barber, the basketball player, and tell him I've talked to his real daddy, who's a dead man overseas. Yeah, why don't I do that. But anyway, today I finally do what I've been coming here to do all week. I stand up and shout into the wind, "Randall! You're not famous! They don't remember you, just like they're not going to remember me! They're voting the graveyard in Moore County, Randall! Your name is still on the party rolls! Every April and every November since you died, you've voted the straight Republican ticket! That's why you're stuck in Singapore, Randall," I shout as the tears begin and the wind fills my mouth, "have a nice day, buddy! Have a goddamned nice day!"

The Biggest Nation

This seat here? No, honey, it's not taken. Just set right down and rest. These malls make me paralyzed tired, don't they you? I'm so tired I'd have to make the walls come to me so I could bump into 'em. I'm Dreama McDonald, by the way, pleased to meet you.

Now, my husband, Floyd, is otherwise. Where clothes is concerned, he'll shop till he drops, and only for the best, that is, when we're in the money: cashmere coats, pinkie rings, silk ties, cuff links. I tell him he buys clothes like they're going out of style.

Floyd's not book smart like my brother Norton, but he's people smart. Wearing a suit and tie to work's kept him out of a lot of dirty jobs. Compared to him, everybody else on the line always looked strictly lower Basin Street. Over at Aeronica they'd see him standing around in a suit and they'd make him Inspector! Why, when I first knew him, people called him the Best-Dressed Man in Dayton, and he didn't even live there anymore. Of course me, I'm a sale person, what with prices higher'n a Georgia pine. Every little bit helps, you know, as the old lady said when she peed in the ocean.

While I'm waiting for Floyd like this, I people watch. Most people aren't out here to buy anything. They're just sashaying, killing time because they accidentally woke up still alive this morning. I learned to people watch when we was with the carnival out west. Honey, you saw everything on the midway, freaks paying to see freaks. And Indians. I'm more of a hangbacker, but Floyd will get acquainted with anybody. There was one old squaw in New Mexico, tits as big as gallon cans, that wanted him to be godfather to her baby. Oh, he gets along with everybody. My powers of acquaintance isn't nothing compared to his, as you would instantly see if you met him.

Now look at that man down there, on the other end of the bench. *Look at that* receding chin and that hair combed straight back from such a low forehead. Don't he look like a possum? Hi there, Possum! No, it's all right, he don't know I'm talking to him.

Mind if I smoke? If you do, you can move. When I was pregnant I quit smoking for a year and a half, and the whole time I saw cigarettes as long as my arm and twice as big around. They're my faithful friends. Who else would get up with me at three in the morning when I get the creepy crawlies from too much thinking? Most of us need all the friends we can get, and in my opinion, whether cigarettes hurt more than they help is a mute point. As Floyd says, you got to die of something. But, now, they didn't have nothing to do with our baby not living.

Yes, I do shop here quite often, especially around the holidays when it's so cheery. After we sold the business we could finally relax like this, but we don't let no moss grow on us like some people. The couple across the hall wears out two decks of playing cards a week on pinochle. Of course, at first we went to the Eagles a lot, but like Floyd says, the trouble with whiskey is, it gets in your stomach so bad. The world don't need two more retired alcoholics.

Later I tried to get him to go down to the Golden Agers with me.

"I ain't setting around with them old farts," says Floyd.

"Why not? You're an old fart," I said, but my logic didn't dent him.

Floyd's always been a party boy, see. You ought to hear him sing "Mammy." One day after we retired, he went out in front of our apartment building and glued a quarter to the sidewalk. Then we invited the couple in 2B over and set at our window for three hours, laughing and watching everybody try to pick it up. About once a month we go to the El Adobe. That Mexican restaurant over on Twenty-fifth and Vine? Floyd doesn't care for foreign food, a steak is the only eat-out food there is for him, but he'll go with me for the taco chips. He has this little gray mouse made of rubber, and he'll put it about half buried in the basket of chips. Then he'll call the waitress over, ask for more chips, and hand her the basket. Taco chips all over the place! Most of the girls is good sports on account of it's Floyd. You'd see right away he's a collector's item.

Now what's Possum laughing about? Look how tickled he is.
Lord, they're going to have to clean his seat!
Well, yes, I'd love for Floyd to meet you too. When he's around,
nobody is lonely and you never know what'll happen—he makes
things happen. Like when we had our little business, he agreed to
sponsor a Republican or a Democrat bowling team, whichever
party won. Right after that we got a telegram from President Nixon
asking for our support in the next election, one of only a hundred
thousand businesses that got one in the state of Ohio. Floyd had it
whatyoucall, xeroxed, and sent it to his brother Bob that thinks
he's shit ice cream and everybody wants a bite. Yes, we was quite up
in the world then, and we've always lived at nice addresses. Why,
right now we live on the same street as the mayor. He lives at
number one-oh-one Grand Avenue and we live at three thousand
seventy-nine. That's exactly right, the Mallview Apartments right
across the highway from here. I can tiptoe over here of a morning
right when she opens. The Imperial's a beautiful car but such a gas
hog, it's not worth it to crank her up. Oh, you better believe it's an
Imperial. We bought that sucker eleven years ago. I never will forget,
one afternoon Floyd come home with $10,000 in cash. "Ask me no
questions and I'll tell you no lies," says Floyd, "but I think we
better turn this into merchandise pretty quick." It's gorgeous, all
white interior. When I'm riding in it I feel like I'm wearing a
wedding dress. It's my friend too, like my cigarettes, and I baby it.
I'd take it to bed with me if I could. My *God*, would you look at
that woman. Now that's what I call a patriotic face: red lipstick,
white powder, blue eye shadow. And she thinks it looks good.
Well, as Floyd always says, the biggest nation is the imagination.
   We got the car when we was living on Easy Street. No joke, there's
an Easy Street in this town. Only two blocks long, which ought to
tell you something about the good life. One time Floyd was drinking Seven and Sevens down at the Eagles and got acquainted with
this lawyer. Pretty soon the lawyer couldn't hit the floor with his hat
and he absolutely refused to believe there was an Easy Street. Floyd
brought him right home. Oh, we had a big time. I fixed him my
Jailhouse Chili, which what else would you feed a lawyer, and we
got to drinking Reds, beer and tomato juice. Come to find out he
was a real important dude and knew Johnny Bench.

We're getting along fine when all of a sudden this lawyer laughs right in Floyd's face. "*Tain't*. You said *tain't,*" he says.

Floyd comes right back at him, "Sure I did. You can't talk as good as me 'cause you didn't go to the same school I did. I speak three languages: literate, illiterate, and profane."

"What school is that?" says the lawyer.

"The school of hard knocks, you simple son of a bitch," Floyd says.

"That's right," I chime in, "we've went all over this great land of ours and known every kind of people: doctors, Mexicans, Mormons. We've got a piece of wood from the Petrified Forest and actual photographs of Mount Rushmore."

"Besides," says Floyd, "I did go through Ohio State. Lots of times, when I drove a delivery truck up in Columbus."

That lawyer just hee-hawed. "I know some people'd get a kick out of meeting you, Floyd. I'll have my secretary send you and your lovely wife an invitation to our family Christmas party," he says.

Which I bought a dress to go to, but the invitation never came. Now if that lawyer trotted up with the invitation, I wouldn't give him yesterday's ice water. Though I did make it my business to see where they lived and what his wife looked like. One time I saw her coming out of their big house, switching her bony little butt. The rich are all crooks anyway. You never have to pay somebody to watch your coat in a cheap restaurant, do you?

Now there goes some boys on cocaine. See the way they're sniffing like they've got a cold? That's how you can tell. Floyd taught me to recognize it. It's a shame what drugs are doing to our young people, and to think it all started with convenience foods. Why, hadn't you figured that out? When I was growing up, the only time we saw an orange was in the toe of our Christmas stocking, and we never had orange juice. I didn't have orange juice until after we was married and Floyd took me to Florida. Now you can buy it frozen for as little as eighty-nine cents a can on sale. Not only that, but you can buy any kind of frozen dinner—Chinese, Italian, French. Speaking of foreign cooking, imagine Floyd and I's surprise when we went to a fancy French restaurant in St. Louis one time and found out all those famous French sauces aren't nothing but gravies. I said, "Lord, honey, all the time we've been eating biscuits and sop, we was enjoying French gourmet food and didn't even know it."

But my point is that convenience foods got people to expecting their tastes to be satisfied too quick. Next come the fast food restaurants, and then the drugs. How many people do you think would snort it up their nose if they had to grow the durned stuff and render it? About as many people as would be eating bacon if they had to kill the hog and cure it. Oh, people are so lazy these days they wouldn't say "sooey" if the hog was eating them up.

That's why I try to do my bit at the holidays for the forgotten ones. Look how many people is sitting in this mall, not waiting for anybody but themselves. There is so many lost souls out there that no one is thinking of, which I decide on Thanksgiving who to invite to Christmas dinner. After they run the Shah of Iran out, and he was wandering from one place to another so sick, I invited him. I invited Nixon too, one of those years when he was in disgrace. After all, he sent us that telegram when he was riding high. There's not no excuse for being lonely if you have a little bit of imagination. We had a big time, me and Nixon and the Shah.

Look, the mall's going to close pretty soon and like I said, I just live over the way. I've had such a pleasant time getting acquainted with you while I was waiting for Floyd. Why don't you come home with me and have supper? I've got some cabbage rolls made from an actual Polish recipe of a man we knew when we was in business. You can help me decide who to invite this Christmas. Pete Rose and Mayor Ed Koch are two I'm considering. And if you're an ax murderer, it don't make a bit of difference. Ax murderers have to eat too, and besides, I stopped worrying about that kind of thing a long time ago. Truthfully it was two years and seven months ago when Floyd was in the hospital for all them tests. We thought it was chronic indigestion due to an ulcer and I'd been feeding him Maalox and ice cream by the bucketful, so we didn't go in till he couldn't keep nothing down for a week. Along about eight-thirty one night his doctor come by with the test results and called me out in the hall. He said this and that which I couldn't understand and then he said a kind of cancerous word and I knew we were in for it.

I must have walked those hospital corridors for two hours before I thought I was calm enough to go back in where Floyd was, but the minute I tried it my heart speeded up till it was ripping along like a lawn mower, and when I looked at him laying there so still, I commenced to cry. Floyd opened his eyes real slow, like raising heavy windows, and he smiled. It was a pale, white smile, like the faint little moon you see in the late afternoon sky sometimes in the winter.

"Come here, Dreama, and lay your head on my shoulder," he said, and I laid down along the edge of the bed and did like he told me.

"Now breathe when I do," he said, and I did, and after a while my heart and my breathing slowed down until they was calm and smooth as a whisper.

"Go to sleep now. Everything will be all right in the morning. I'm just so tired," Floyd said, and kissed my forehead.

And I've been coming here ever since.

Elaine Fowler Palencia, a freelance writer living in Champaign, Illinois, grew up in Kentucky and Tennessee. Writing as Laurel Blake, she is the author of several romance novels and was a finalist for the Golden Medallion Award of the Romance Writers of America. Her short stories have appeared in *Iowa Woman, Crescent Review,* and other literary magazines.